# VOICES IN THE NIGHT:
# RARE STORIES

# VOICES IN THE NIGHT: RARE STORIES

## WILLIAM HOPE HODGSON

**WORLD LIBRARY CLASSICS**

**VOICES IN THE NIGHT: RARE STORIES**

Published by WLC BOOKS.

# CONTENTS

# THE DERELICT

"IT'S the *material*," said the old ship's doctor — "the *material* plus the conditions — and, maybe," he added slowly, "a third factor — yes, a third factor; but there, there —" He broke off his half-meditative sentence and began to charge his pipe.

"Go on, doctor," we said encouragingly, and with more than a little expectancy. We were in the smoke-room of the Sand-a-lea, running across the North Atlantic; and the doctor was a character. He concluded the charging of his pipe, and lit it; then settled himself, and began to express himself more fully.

"The *material*," he said with conviction, "is inevitably the medium of expression of the life-force — the fulcrum, as it were; lacking which it is unable to exert itself, or, indeed, to express itself in any form or fashion that would be intelligible or evident to us. So potent is the share of the *material* in the production of that thing which we name life, and so eager the life-force to express itself, that I am convinced it would, if given the right conditions, make itself manifest even through so hopeless seeming a medium as a simple block of sawn wood; for I tell you, gentlemen, the life-force is both as fiercely urgent and as indiscriminate as fire — the destructor; yet which some are now growing to consider the very essence of life rampant. There is a quaint seeming paradox there," he concluded, nodding his old grey head.

"Yes, doctor," I said. "In brief, your argument is that life is a thing, state, fact, or element, call it what you like, which requires the *material* through which to manifest itself, and that given the *material*, plus the conditions, the result is life. In other words, that life is an evolved product, manifested through matter and bred of conditions — eh?"

"As we understand the word," said the old doctor. "Though, mind you, there may be a third factor. But, in my heart, I believe that it is a matter of chemistry — conditions and a suitable medium; but given the conditions, the brute is so almighty that it will seize upon anything through which to manifest itself. It is a force generated by conditions; but, nevertheless, this does not bring us one iota nearer to its explanation, any more than to the explanation of electricity or fire. They are, all three, of the outer forces — monsters of the void. Nothing we can do will *create* any one of them, our power is merely to be able, by providing the conditions, to make each one of them manifest to our physical senses. Am I clear?"

"Yes, doctor, in a way, you are," I said. "But I don't agree with you, though I think I understand you. Electricity and fire are both what I might call natural things, but life is an abstract something — a kind of all-permeating wakefulness. Oh, I can't explain it! Who could? But it s spiritual, not just a thing bred out of a condition, like fire, as you say, or electricity. It's a horrible thought of yours. Life's a kind of spiritual mystery —"

"Easy, my boy!" said the old doctor, laughing gently to himself. "Or else I may be asking you to demonstrate the spiritual mystery of life of the limpet, or the crab, shall we say." He grinned at me with ineffable perverseness. "Anyway," he continued, "as I suppose you've all guessed, I've a yarn to tell you in support of my impression that life is no more a mystery or a miracle than fire or electricity. But, please to remember, gentlemen, that because we've succeeded in naming and making good use of these two forces, they're just as much mysteries, fundamentally as ever. And, anyway, the thing I'm going to tell you won't explain the mystery of life, but only give you one of my pegs on which I hang my feeling that life is as I have said, a force made manifest through conditions — that is to say, natural chemistry — and that it can take for its purpose and need, the most incredible and unlikely matter; for without matter it cannot come into existence — it cannot become manifest —"

"I don't agree with you, doctor," I interrupted. "Your theory would destroy all belief in life after death. It would —"

"Hush, sonny," said the old man, with a quiet little smile of comprehension. "Hark to what I've to say first; and, anyway, what objection have you to material life after death? And if you object to a material framework, I would still have you remember that I am speaking of life, as we understand the word in this our life. Now do be a quiet lad, or I'll never be done:

"It was when I was a young man, and that is a good many years ago, gentlemen. I had passed my examinations, but was so run down with overwork that it was decided that I had better take a trip to sea. I was by no means well off, and very glad in the end to secure a nominal post as doctor in the sailing passenger clipper running out to China.

"The name of the ship was the Bheospse, and soon after I had got all my gear aboard she cast off, and we dropped down the Thames, and next day were well away out in the Channel.

"The captain's name was Gannington, a very decent man, though quite illiterate. The first mate, Mr. Berlies, was a quiet, sternish, reserved man, very well-read. The second mate, Mr. Selvern, was, perhaps, by birth and upbringing, the most socially cultured of the three, but he lacked the stamina and indomitable pluck of the two others. He was more of a sensitive, and emotionally and even mentally, the most alert man of the three.

"On our way out, we called at Madagascar, where we landed some of our passengers; then we ran eastward, meaning to call at North-West Cape; but about a hundred degrees east we encountered very dreadful weather, which carried away all our sails, and sprung the jibboom and foret'gallantmast.

"The storm carried us northward for several hundred miles, and when it dropped us finally, we found ourselves in a very bad state. The ship had been strained, and had taken some three feet of water through her seams; the maintopmast had been sprung, in addition to the jibboom and foret'gallantmast, two of our boats had gone, as also one of the pig-stys, with three fine pigs, these latter having been washed overboard but some half-hour before the wind began to ease, which it did very quickly, though a very ugly sea ran for some hours after.

"The wind left us just before dark, and when morning came it brought splendid weather — a calm, mildly undulating sea, and a brilliant sun, with no wind. It showed us also that we were not alone, for about two miles away to the westward was another vessel, which Mr. Selvern, the second mate, pointed out to me.

" 'That's a pretty rum-looking, packet, doctor,' he said, and handed me his glass.

"I looked through it at the other vessel, and saw what he meant; at least, I thought I did.

" 'Yes, Mr. Selvern,' I said. 'She's got a pretty old-fashioned look about her.'

"He laughed at me in his pleasant way.

" 'It's easy to see you're not a sailor, doctor,' he remarked. 'There's a dozen rum things about her. She's a derelict, and has been floating round, by the look of her, for many a score of years. Look at the shape of her counter, and the bows and cutwater. She's as old as the hills, as you might say, and ought to have gone down to Davy Jones a good while ago. Look at the growths on her, and the thickness of her standing rig-ging; that's all salt encrustations, I fancy, if you notice the white colour. She's been a small barque; but, don't you see, she's not a yard left aloft. They've all dropped out of the slings; everything rotted away; wonder the standing rigging hasn't gone, too. I wish the old man would let us take the boat and have a look at her. She'd be well worth it.'

" 'There seemed little chance, however, of this, for all hands were turned to and kept hard at it all day long repairing the damage to the masts and gear; and this took a long while, as you may think. Part of the time I gave a hand heaving on one of the deck capstans, for the exercise was good for my liver. Old Captain Gannington approved, and I persuaded him to come along and try some of the same medicine, which he did; and we got very chummy over the job.

"We got talking about the derelict, and he remarked how lucky we were not to have run full tilt on to her in the darkness, for she lay right away to leeward of us, according, to the way that we had been drifting in the storm. He also was of the opinion that she had a strange look about her, and that she was pretty old; but on this latter point he plainly had far less knowledge than the second mate, for he was, as I have said, an illiterate man, and knew nothing of seacraft beyond what experience had taught him. He lacked the book knowledge which the second mate had of vessels previous to his day, which it appeared the derelict was.

" 'She's an old 'un, doctor,' was the extent of observations in this direction.

"Yet, when I mentioned to him that it would be interesting to go aboard and give her a bit of an overhaul, he nodded his head as if the idea had been already in his mind and accorded with his own inclinations.

" 'When the work's over, doctor,' he said. 'Can't spare the men now, ye know. Got to get all shipshape an' ready as smart as we can. But, we'll take my gig, an' go off in the second dog-watch. The glass is steady, an' it'll be a bit of gam for us.'

"That evening, after tea, the captain gave orders to clear the gig and get her overboard. The second mate was to come with us, and the skipper gave him word to see that two or three lamps were put into the boat, as it would soon fall dark. A little later we were pulling across the calmness of the sea with a crew of six at the oars, and making very good speed of it.

"Now, gentlemen, I have detailed to you with great exactness all the facts, both big and little, so that you can follow step by step each incident in this extraordinary affair, and I want you now to pay the closest attention. I was sitting in the stern-sheets with the second mate and the captain, who was steering, and as we drew nearer and nearer to the stranger I studied her with an ever-growing attention, as, indeed, did Captain Gannington and the second mate. She was, as you know, to the west-ward of us, and the sunset was making a great flame of red light to the back of her, so that she showed a little blurred and indistinct by reason of the halation of the light, which almost defeated the eye in any attempt to see her rotting spars and standing rigging, submerged, as they were, in the fiery glory of the sunset.

"It was because of this effect of the sunset that we had come quite close, comparatively, to the derelict before we saw that she was all surrounded by a sort of curious scum, the colour of which was difficult to decide upon by reason of the red light that was in the atmosphere, but which afterwards we discovered to be brown. This scum spread all about the old vessel for many hundreds of yards in a huge, irregular patch, a great stretch of which reached out to the eastward, upon the starboard side of the boat some score or so fathoms away.

" 'Queer stuff,' said Captain Gannington, leaning to the side and looking over. 'Something in the cargo as 'as gone rotten, and worked out through 'er seams.'

" 'Look at her bows and stern,' said the second mate. 'Just look at the growth on her!'

"There were, as he said, great clumpings of strange-looking sea-fungi under the bows and the short counter astern. From the stump of her jibboom and her cutwater great beards of rime and marine growths hung downward into the scum that held her in. Her blank starboard side was presented to us — all a dead, dirtyish white, streaked and mottled vaguely with dull masses of heavier colour.

"'There's a steam or haze rising off her,' said the second mate, speaking again. 'You can see it against the light. It keeps coming and going. Look!'

"I saw then what he meant — a faint haze or steam, either suspended above the old vessel or rising from her. And Captain Gannington saw it also.

" 'Spontaneous combustion!' he exclaimed. 'We'll 'ave to watch when we lift the 'atches, 'nless it's some poor devil that's got aboard of 'er. But that ain't likely.'

"We were now within a couple of hundred yards of the old derelict, and had entered into the brown scum. As it poured off the lifted oars I heard one of the men mutter to himself, 'Dam' treacle!' And, indeed, it was not something unlike it. As the boat continued to forge nearer and nearer to the old ship the scum grew thicker and thicker, so that, at last, it perceptibly slowed us.

" 'Give way, lads! Put some beef to it!' sang out Captain Gannington. And thereafter there was no sound except the panting of the men and the faint, reiterated suck, suck of the sullen brown scum upon the oars as the boat was forced ahead. As we went, I was conscious of a peculiar smell in the evening air, and whilst I had no doubt that the puddling of the scum by the oars made it rise, I could give no name to it; yet, in a way, it was vaguely familiar.

"We were now very close to the old vessel, and presently she was high about us against the dying light. The captain called out then to 'in with the bow oars and stand by with the boat-hook,' which was done.

" 'Aboard there! Ahoy! Aboard there! Ahoy!' shouted Captain Gannington; but there came no answer, only the dull sound his voice going lost into the open sea, each time he sung out.

" 'Ahoy! Aboard there! Ahoy!' he shouted time after time, but there was only the weary silence of the old hulk that answered us; and, somehow as he shouted, the while that I stared up half expectantly at her, a queer little sense of oppression, that amounted almost to nervousness, came upon me. It passed, but I remember how I was suddenly aware that it was growing dark. Darkness comes fairly rapidly in the tropics, though not so quickly as many fiction writers seem to think; but it was not that the coming dusk had perceptibly deepened in that brief time of only a few moments, but rather that my nerves had made me suddenly a little hypersensitive. I mention my state particularly, for I am not a nervy man normally, and my abrupt touch of nerves is significant, in the light of what happened.

" 'There's no one on board there!' said Captain Gannington. 'Give way, men!' For the boat's crew had instinctively rested on their oars, as the captain hailed the old craft. The men gave way again; and then the second mate called out excitedly, 'Why, look there, there's our pigsty! See, it's got Bheospse painted on the end. It's drifted down here and the scum's caught it. What a blessed wonder!'

"It was, as he had said, our pigsty that had been washed overboard in the storm; and most extraordinary to come across it there.

" 'We'll tow it off with us, when we go,' said the captain, and shouted to the crew to get down to their oars; for they were hardly moving the boat, because the scum was so thick, close in around the old ship, that it literally clogged the boat from moving. I remember that it struck me, in a half-conscious sort of way, as curious that the pigsty, containing our three dead pigs, had managed to drift in so far unaided, whilst we could scarcely manage to force the boat in, now that we had come right into the scum. But the thought passed from my mind, for so many things happened within the next few minutes.

"The men managed to bring the boat in alongside, within a couple of feet of the derelict, and the man with the boat-hook hooked on.

" ''Ave ye got 'old there, forrard?' asked Captain Gannington.

" 'Yessir!' said the bowman; and as he spoke there came a queer noise of tearing.

" 'What's that?' asked the Captain.

" 'It's tore, sir. Tore clean away!' said the man, and his tone showed that he had received something of a shock.

" 'Get a hold again, then!' said Captain Gannington irritably. 'You don't s'pose this packet was built yesterday! Shove the hook into the main chains' The man did so gingerly, as you might say, for it seemed to me, in the growing dusk, that he put no strain on to the hook, though, of course there was no need — you see the boat could not go very far of herself, in the stuff in which she was imbedded. I remember thinking this, also as I looked up at the bulging side of the old vessel. Then I heard Captain Gannington's voice:

" 'Lord, but she s old! An' what a colour, doctor! She don't half want paint, do she? Now then, somebody, one of them oars.' An oar was passed to him, and he leant it up against the ancient, bulging side; then he paused, and called to the second mate to light a couple of the lamps, and stand by to pass them up, for darkness had settled down now upon the sea.

"The second mate lit two of the lamps, and told one of the men to light a third, and keep it handy in the boat; then he stepped across, with a lamp in each hand, to where Captain Gannington stood by the oar against the side of the ship.

" 'Now, my lad,' said the captain to the man who had pulled stroke, 'up with you, an' we'll pass ye up the lamps.'

"The man jumped to obey, caught the oar, and put his weight upon it; and as he did so, something seemed to give way a little.

" 'Look!' cried out the second mate, and pointed, lamp in hand. 'It's sunk in!'

"This was true. The oar had made quite an indentation into the bulging, somewhat slimy side of the old vessel.

" 'Mould, I reckon,' said Captain Gannington, bending towards the derelict to look. Then to the man:

" 'Up you go, my lad, and be smart! Don't stand there waitin'!'

"At that the man, who had paused a moment as he felt the oar give beneath his weight began to shin' up, and in a few seconds he was aboard, and leant out over the rail for the lamps. These were passed up to him, and the captain called to him to steady the oar. Then Captain Gannington went, calling to me to follow, and after me the second mate.

"As the captain put his face over the rail, he gave a cry of astonishment.

" 'Mould, by gum! Mould — tons of it. Good lord!'

"As I heard him shout that I scrambled the more eagerly after him, and in a moment or two I was able to see what he meant — everywhere that the light from the two lamps struck there was nothing but smooth great masses and surfaces of a dirty white coloured mould. I climbed over the rail, with the second mate close behind, and stood upon the mould covered decks. There might have been no planking beneath the mould, for all that our feet could feel. It gave under our tread with a spongy, puddingy feel. It covered the deck furniture of the old ship, so that the shape of each article and fitment was often no more than suggested through it.

"Captain Gannington snatched a lamp from the man and the second mate reached for the other. They held the lamps high, and we all stared. It was most extraordinary, and somehow most abominable. I can think of no other word, gentlemen, that so much describes the predominant feeling that affected me at the moment.

" 'Good lord!' said Captain Gannington several times. 'Good lord!' But neither the second mate nor the man said anything, and, for my part I just stared, and at the same time began to smell a little at the air, for there was a vague odour of something half familiar, that somehow brought to me a sense of half-known fright.

"I turned this way and that, staring, as I have said. Here and there the mould was so heavy as to entirely disguise what lay beneath, converting the deck-fittings into indistinguishable mounds of mould all dirty-white and blotched and veined with irregular, dull, purplish markings.

"There was a strange thing about the mould which Captain Gannington drew attention to — it was that our feet did not crush into it and break the surface, as might have been expected, but merely indented it.

" 'Never seen nothin' like it before! Never!' said the captain after having stooped with his lamp to examine the mould under our feet. He stamped with his heel, and the mould gave out a dull, puddingy sound. He stooped again, with a quick movement, and stared, holding the lamp close to the deck. 'Blest if it ain't a reg'lar skin to it!'

"The second mate and the man and I all stooped and looked at it. The second mate progged it with his forefinger, and I remember I rapped it several times with my knuckles, listening to the dead sound it gave out, and noticing the close, firm texture of the mould.

" 'Dough!' the second mate. 'It's just like blessed dough! Pouf!' He stood up with a quick movement. 'I could fancy it stinks a bit,' he said.

"As he said this I knew, suddenly, what the familiar thing was in the vague odour that hung about us — it was that the smell had something animal-like in it; something of the same smell, only *heavier*, that you would smell in any place that is infested with mice. I began to look about with a sudden very real uneasiness. There might be vast numbers of hungry rats aboard. They might prove exceedingly dangerous, if in a starving condition; yet, as you will understand, somehow I hesitated to put forward my idea as a reason for caution, it was too fanciful.

"Captain Gannington had begun to go aft along the mould-covered main-deck with the second mate, each of them holding their lamps high up, so as to cast a good light about the vessel. I turned quickly and followed them, the man with me keeping close to my heels, and plainly uneasy. As we went, I became aware that there was a feeling of moisture in the air, and I remembered the slight mist, or smoke, above the hulk, which had made Captain Gannington suggest spontaneous combustion in explanation.

"And always, as we went, there was that vague, animal smell; suddenly I found myself wishing we were well away from the old vessel.

"Abruptly, after a few paces, the captain stopped and pointed at a row of mould-hidden shapes on each side of the maindeck. 'Guns,' he said. 'Been a privateer in the old days, I guess — maybe worse! We'll 'ave a look below, doctor; there may be something worth touchin'. She's older than I thought. Mr. Selvern thinks she's about two hundred years old; but I scarce think it.'

"We continued our way aft, and I remember that I found myself walking as lightly and gingerly as possible, as if I were subconsciously afraid of treading through the rotten, mould-hid decks. I think the others had a touch of the same feeling, from the way that they walked. Occasionally the soft stuff would grip our heels, releasing them with a little sullen suck.

"The captain forged somewhat ahead of the second mate; and I know that the suggestion he had made himself, that perhaps there might be something below worth carrying away, had stimulated his imagination. The second mate was, however, beginning to feel somewhat the same way that I did; at least I have that impression. I think, if it had not been for what I might truly describe as Captain Gannington's sturdy courage, we should all of us have just gone back over the side very soon, for there was most certainly an unwholesome feeling abroad that made one feel queerly lacking in pluck; and you will soon see that this feeling was justified.

"Just as the captain reached the few mould-covered steps leading up on to the short half-poop, I was suddenly aware that the feeling of moisture in the air had grown very much more definite. It was perceptible now, intermittently, as a sort of thin, moist, fog-like vapour, that came and went oddly, and seemed to make the decks a little indistinct to the view, this time and that. Once an odd puff of it beat up suddenly from somewhere, and caught me in the face, carrying a queer, sickly, heavy odour with it that somehow frightened me strangely with a suggestion of a waiting and half-comprehended danger.

"We had followed Captain Gannington up the three mould covered steps, and now went slowly along the raised after-deck. By the mizzen-mast Captain Gannington paused, and held his lantern near to it. 'My word, mister,' he said to the second mate, 'it's fair thickened up with mould! Why, I'll g'antee it's close on four foot thick.' He shone the light down to where it met the deck. 'Good lord!' he said. 'Look at the sea-lice on it!' I stepped up, and it was as he had said; the sea-lice were thick upon it, some of them huge, not less than the size of large beetles, and all a clear, colourless shade, like water, except where there were little spots of grey on them.

" 'I've never seen the like of them, 'cept on a live cod,' said Captain Gannington, in an extremely puzzled voice. 'My word! But they're whoppers!' Then he passed on; but a few paces farther aft he stopped again, and held his lamp near to the mould-hidden deck.

" 'Lord bless me, doctor,' he called out, in a low voice, 'did ye ever see the like of that? Why, it's a foot long, if it's a hinch!'

"I stooped over his shoulder, and saw what he meant; it was a clear, colourless creature about a foot long, and about eight inches high, with a curved back that was extraordinarily narrow. As we stared, all in a group, it gave a queer little flick, and was gone.

" 'Jumped!' said the captain. 'Well, if that ain't a giant of all the sea-lice that ever I've seen. I guess it's jumped twenty foot clear.' He straightened his back, and scratched his head a moment, swinging the lantern this way and that with the other hand, and staring about us. 'Wot are *they* doin' aboard 'ere?' he said. 'You'll see 'em — little things — on fat cod an' such-like. I'm blowed, doctor, if I understand.'

"He held his lamp towards a big mound of the mould that occupied part of the after portion of the low poop-deck, a little foreside of where there came a two-foot high 'break' to a kind of second and loftier poop, that ran away aft to the taffrail. The mound was pretty big, several feet across, and more than a yard high. Captain Gannington walked up to it.

" 'I reck'n this's the scuttle,' he remarked, and gave it a heavy kick. The only result was a deep indentation into the huge, whiteish hump of mould, as if he had driven his foot into a mass of some doughy substance. Yet I am not altogether correct in saying that this was the only result, for a certain other thing happened. From the place made by the captain's foot there came a sudden gush of a purplish fluid, accompanied by a peculiar smell, that was, and was not, half familiar. Some of the mould-like substance had stuck to the toe of the captain's boot, and from this likewise there issued a sweat, as it were, of the same colour.

" 'Well?' said Captain Gannington, in surprise, and drew back his foot to make another kick at the hump of mould. But he paused at an exclamation from the second mate:

" 'Don't sir,' said the second mate.

"I glanced at him, and the light from Captain Gannington's lamp showed me that his face had a bewildered, half-frightened look, as if he were suddenly and unexpectedly half afraid of something, and as if his tongue had given away his sudden fright, without any intention on his part to speak. The captain also turned and stared at him.

" 'Why, mister?' he asked, in a somewhat puzzled voice, through which there sounded just the vaguest hint of annoyance. 'We've got to shift this muck, if we're to get below.'

"I looked at the second mate, and it seemed to me that, curiously enough he was listening less to the captain than to some other sound. Suddenly he said, in a queer voice, 'Listen, everybody!'

"Yet we heard nothing, beyond the faint murmur of the men talking together in the boat alongside.

" 'I don't, hear nothing,' said Captain Gannington, after a short pause. 'Do you, doctor?'

" 'No,' I said.

" 'Wot was it you thought you heard?' the captain, turning again to the second mate. But the second mate shook his head in a curious, almost irritable way, as if the captain's question interrupted his listening. Captain Gannington stared a moment at him, then held his lantern up and glanced about him almost uneasily. I know I felt a queer sense of strain. But the light showed nothing beyond the greyish dirty-white of the mould in all directions.

" 'Mister Selvern,' said the captain, at last, looking at him, 'don't get fancying, things. Get hold of your bloomin' self. Ye know ye heard nothin'?'

" 'I'm quite sure I heard something, sir,' said the second mate. 'I seemed to hear —' He broke off sharply, and appeared to listen with an almost painful intensity.

" 'What did it sound like?' I asked.

" 'It's all right, doctor,' said Captain Gannington, laughing gently. 'Ye can give him a tonic when we get back. I'm goin' to shift this stuff.' He drew back, and kicked for the second time at the ugly mass which he took to hide the companionway. The result of his kick was startling, for the whole thing wobbled sloppily, like a mound of unhealthy-looking jelly.

"He drew his foot out of it quickly, and took a step backward, staring, and holding his lamp towards it. 'By gum,' he said, and it was plain that he was generally startled, 'the blessed thing's gone soft!'

"The man had run back several steps from the suddenly flaccid mound, and looking horribly frightened. Though of what, I am sure he had not the least idea. The second mate stood where he was, and stared. For my part, I know I had a most hideous uneasiness upon me. The captain continued to hold his light towards the wobbling mound and stare.

" 'It's gone squashy all through,' he said. 'There's no scuttle there. There's no bally woodwork inside that lot! Phoo! What a rum smell!'

"He walked round to the after side of the strange mound, to see whether there might be some signs of an opening, into the hull at the back of the great heap of mould-stuff. And then:

" 'Listen!' said the second mate again, in the strangest sort of voice.

"Captain Gannington straightened himself upright, and there succeeded a pause of the most intense quietness, in which there was not even the hum of talk from the men alongside in the boat. We all heard it — a kind of dull, soft thud, thud, thud, thud, somewhere in the hull under us, yet so vague as to make me half doubtful I heard it, only that the others did so, too.

"Captain Gannington turned suddenly to where the man stood.

" 'Tell them —' he began. But the fellow cried out something, and pointed. There had come a strange intensity into his somewhat unemotional face, so that the captain's glance followed his action instantly. I stared also as you may think. It was the great mound at which the man was pointing. I saw what he meant. From the two gapes made in the mould-like stuff by Captain Gannington's boot, the purple fluid was jetting out in a queerly regular fashion, almost as if it were being forced out by a pump. My word! But I stared! And even as I stared a larger jet squirted out, and splashed as far as the man, spattering his boots and trouser legs.

"The fellow had been pretty nervous before, in a stolid, ignorant sort of way, and his funk had been growing steadily; but at this he simply let out a yell, and turned about to run. He paused an instant,as if a sudden fear of the darkness that held the decks, between him and the boat, had taken him. He snatched at the second mate's lantern, tore it out of his hand, and plunged heavily away over the vile stretch of mould.

"Mr. Selvern, the second mate, said not a word; he was just staring,

staring at the strange-smelling twin-streams of dull purple that were jetting out from the wobbling mound. Captain Gannington, however, roared an order to the man to come back, but the man plunged on and on across the mould, his feet seeming to be clogged by the stuff, as if it had grown suddenly soft. He zigzagged as he ran, the lantern swaying, in wild circles as he wrenched his feet free with a constant plop, plop; and I could hear his frightened gasps even from where I stood.

" 'Come back with that lamp!' roared the captain again; but still the man took no notice.

"And Captain Gannington was silent an instant, his lips working in a queer, inarticulate fashion, as if he were stunned momentarily by the very violence of his anger at the man's insubordination. And in the silence I heard the sounds again — thud, thud, thud, thud! Quite distinctly now, beating, it seemed suddenly to me, right down under my feet, but deep.

"I stared down at the mould on which I was standing, with a quick, disgusting sense of the terrible all about me; then I looked at the captain, and tried to say something, without appearing frightened. I saw that he had turned again to the mound, and all the anger had gone out of his face. He had his lamp out towards the mound, and was listening. There was another moment of absolute silence, at least, I knew that I was not conscious of any sound at all in all the world, except that extraordinary thud, thud, thud, thud, down somewhere in the huge bulk under us.

"The captain shifted his feet with a sudden, nervous movement, and as he lifted them the mould went plop, plop! He looked quickly at me, trying to smile, as if he were not thinking anything very much about it.

" 'What do you make of it, doctor?' he said.

" 'I think —' I began. But the second mate interrupted with a single word, his voice pitched a little high, in a tone that made us both stare instantly at him.

" 'Look!' he said, and pointed at the mound. The thing was all of a slow quiver. A strange ripple ran outward from it, along the deck, like you will see a ripple run inshore out of a calm sea. It reached a mound a little foreside of us, which I had supposed to be the cabin skylight, and in a moment the second mound sank nearly level with the surrounding decks, quivering floppily in a most extraordinary fashion. A sudden quick tremor took the mould right under the second mate, and he gave out a hoarse little cry, and held his arms out on each side of him, to keep his balance. The tremor in the mould spread, and Captain Gannington swayed, and spread out his feet with a sudden curse of fright. The second mate jumped across to him, and caught him by the wrist.

" 'The boat, sir!' he said, saying the very thing that I had lacked the pluck to say. 'For God's sake —'

"But he never finished, for a tremendous hoarse scream cut off his words. They hove themselves round and looked. I could see without turning. The man who had run from us was standing in the waist of the ship, about a fathom from the starboard bulwarks. He was swaying from side to side, and screaming, in a dreadful fashion. He appeared to be trying to lift his feet, and the light from his swaying lantern showed an almost incredible sight. All about him the mould was in active movement. His feet had sunk out of sight. The stuff appeared to be *lapping* at his legs and abruptly his bare flesh showed. The hideous stuff had rent his trouser-leg away as if it were paper. He gave out a simply sickening scream, and, with a vast effort, wrenched one leg free. It was partly destroyed. The next instant he pitched face downward, and the stuff heaped itself upon him, as if it were actually alive, with a dreadful, severe life. It was simply infernal. The man had gone from sight. Where he had fallen was now a writhing, elongated mound, in constant and horrible increase, as the mould appeared to move towards it in strange ripples from all sides.

"Captain Gannington and the second mate were stone silent, in amazed and incredulous horror, but I had begun to reach towards a grotesque and terrific conclusion, both helped and hindered by my professional training.

"From the men in the boat alongside there was a loud shouting. and I saw two of their faces appear suddenly above the rail. They showed clearly a moment in the light from the lamp which the man had snatched from Mr. Selvern; for, strangely enough, this lamp was standing upright and unharmed on the deck, a little way foreside of that dreadful, elongated, growing mound, that still swayed and writhed with an incredible horror. The lamp rose and fell on the passing ripples of the mould, just — for all the world — as you will see a boat rise and fall on little swells. It is of some interest to me now, psychologically, to remember how that rising and falling lantern brought home to me more than anything the incomprehensible dreadful strangeness of it all.

"The men's faces disappeared with sudden yells, as if they had slipped, or been suddenly hurt; and there was a fresh uproar of shouting from the boat. The men were calling to us to come away — to come away. In the same instant I felt my left boot drawn suddenly and forcibly downward, with a horrible, painful grip. I wrenched it free, with a yell of angry fear. Forrard of us, I saw that the vile surface was all amove, and abruptly I found myself shouting in a queer, frightened voice, 'The boat, captain! The boat, captain!'

"Captain Gannington stared round at me, over his right shoulder, in a peculiar, dull way, that told me he was utterly dazed with bewilderment and the incomprehensibleness of it all. I took a quick, clogged, nervous step towards him, and gripped his arm, and shook it fiercely. 'The boat!' I shouted at him. 'The boat! For God's sake, tell the men to bring the boat aft!'

"Then the mound must have drawn his feet down, for abruptly he bellowed fiercely with terror, his momentary apathy giving place to furious energy. His thickset, vastly muscular body doubled and writhed with his enormous effort, and he struck out madly dropping the lantern. He tore his feet free, something ripping as he did so. The *reality* and necessity of the situation had come upon him brutishly real, and he was roaring to the men in the boat, 'Bring the boat aft! Bring 'er aft! Bring 'er aft!' The second mate and I were shouting the same thing madly.

" 'For God's sake, be smart, lads!' roared the captain, and stooped quickly for his lamp, which still burned. His feet were gripped again, and he hove them out, blaspheming breathlessly, aud leaping a yard high with his effort. Then he made a run for the side, wrenching his feet free at each step. In the same instant the second mate cried out something, and grabbed at the captain.

" 'It's got hold of my feet! It's got hold of my feet!' he screamed. His feet, had disappeared up to his boot-tops, and Captain Gannington caught him round the waist with his powerful left arm, gave a mighty heave, and the next instant had him free; but both his boot-soles had gone. For my part, I jumped madly from foot to foot, to avoid the plucking of the mould; and suddenly I made a run for the ship's side. But before I could get there, a queer gape came in the mould between us and the side, at least a couple of feet wide, and how deep I don't know. It closed up in an instant, and all the mould where the cape had been vent into a sort of flurry of horrible ripplings, so that I ran back from it; for I did not dare to put my foot upon it. Then the captain was shouting to me:

" 'Aft, doctor! Aft, doctor! This way, doctor! Run!' I saw then that he had passed me, and was up on the after raised portion of the poop. He had the second mate, thrown like a sack, all loose and quiet, over his left shoulder; for Mr. Selvern had fainted, and his long legs flogged limp and helpless against the captain's massive knees as he ran. I saw, with a queer, unconscious noting of minor details, how the torn soles of the second mate's boots flapped and jigged as the captain staggered aft.

" 'Boat ahoy! Boat ahoy! Boat ahoy!' shouted the captain; and then I was beside him, shouting also. The men were answering with loud yells of encouragement, and it was plain they were working desperately to force the boat aft through the thick scum about the ship.

"We reached the ancient, mould-hid taffrail, and slewed about breathlessly in the half-darkness to see what was happening. Captain Gannington had left his lantern by the big mound when he picked up the second mate; and as we stood, gasping we discovered suddenly that all the mould between us and the light was full of movement. Yet, the part on which we stood, for about six or eight feet forrard of us, was still firm.

"Every couple of seconds we shouted to the men to hasten, and they kept on calling to us that they would be with us in an instant. And all the time we watched the deck of that dreadful hulk, feeling, for my part, literally sick with mad suspense, and ready to jump overboard into that filthy scum all about us.

"Down somewhere in the huge bulk of the ship there was all the time that extraordinary dull, ponderous thud, thud, thud, thud growing ever louder. I seemed to feel the whole hull of the derelict, beginning to quiver and thrill with each dull beat. And to me, with the grotesque and hideous suspicion of what made that noise, it was at once the most dreadful and incredible sound I have ever heard.

"As we waited desperately for the boat, I scanned incessantly so much of the grey white bulk as the lamp showed. The whole of the decks seemed to be in strange movement. Forrard of the lamp, I could see indistinctly the moundings of the mould swaying and nodding hideously beyond the circle of the brightest rays. Nearer, and full in the glow of the lamp, the mound which should have indicated the skylight, was swelling steadily. There were ugly, purple veinings on it, and as it swelled, it seemed to me that the veinings and mottlings on it were becoming plainer, rising as though embossed upon it, like you will see the veins stand out on the body of a powerful, full-blooded horse. It was most extraordinary. The mound that we had supposed to cover the companionway had sunk flat with the surrounding mould, and I could not see that it jetted out any more of the purplish fluid.

"A quaking movement of the mound began away forrard of the lamp, and came flurrying away aft towards us, and at the sight of that I climbed up on to the spongy-feeling taffrail, and yelled afresh for the boat. The men answered with a shout, which told me they were nearer, but the beastly scum was so thick that it was evidently a fight to move the boat at all. Beside me, Captain Gannington was shaking the second mate furiously, and the man stirred and began to moan. The captain shook him again, 'Wake up! Wake up, mister!' he shouted.

"The second mate staggered out of the captain's arms, and collapsed suddenly, shrieking: 'My feet! Oh, God! My feet!' The captain and I lugged him off the mound, and got him into a sitting position upon the taffrail, where he kept up a continual moaning.

" 'Hold 'im, doctor,' said the captain. And whilst I did so, he ran for-rard a few yards, and peered down over the starboard quarter rail. 'For God's sake, be smart, lads! Be smart! Be smart!' he shouted down to the men, and they answered him, breathless, from close at hand, yet still too far away for the boat to be any use to us on the instant.

"I was holding the moaning, half-unconscious officer, and staring forrard along the poop decks. The flurrying of the mould was coming aft, slowly and noiselessly. And then, suddenly, I saw something clos-er:

" 'Look out, captain!' I shouted. And even as I shouted, the mould near to him gave a sudden, peculiar slobber. I had seen a ripple stealing towards him through the mould. He gave an enormous, clumsy leap, and landed near to us on the sound part of the mould, but the movement followed him. He turned and faced it, swearing fiercely. All about his feet there came abruptly little gapings, which made horrid sucking nois-es. 'Come back, captain!' I yelled. 'Come back, *quick!*' As I shouted, a ripple came at his feet — lipping at them; and he stamped insanely at it, and leaped back, his boot torn half off his foot. He swore madly with pain and anger, and jumped swiftly for the taffrail.

" 'Come on, doctor! Over we go!' he called. Then he remembered the filthy scum, and hesitated, and roared out desperately to the men to hurry. I stared down, also.

" 'The second mate?' I said.

" 'I'll take charge doctor,' said Captain Gannington, and caught hold of Mr. Selvern. As he spoke, I thought I saw something beneath us, outlined against the scum. I leaned out over the stern, and peered. There was something under the port-quarter.

" 'There's something down there, captain!' I called, and pointed in the darkness. He stooped far over, and stared.

" 'A boat, by gum! A *boat!*' he yelled, and began to wriggle swiftly along the taffrail, dragging the second mate after him. I followed. 'A boat it is, sure!' he exclaimed a few moments later, and, picking up the second mate clear of the rail, he hove him down into the boat, where he fell with a crash into the bottom.

" 'Over ye go, doctor!' he yelled at me, and pulled me bodily off the rail and dropped me after the officer. As he did so, I felt the whole of the ancient, spongy rail give a peculiar, sickening quiver, and begin to wobble. I fell on to the second mate, and the captain came after, almost in the same instant, but, fortunately, he landed clear of us, on to the fore thwart, which broke under his weight, with a loud crack and splintering of wood.

" 'Thank God!' I heard him mutter. 'Thank God! I guess that was a mighty near thing to going to Hades.'

"He struck a match, just as I got to my feet, and between us we got the second mate straightened out on one of the after fore-and-aft thwarts. We shouted to the men in the boat, telling them where we were, and saw the light of their lantern shining round the starboard counter of the derelict. They called back to us to tell us they were doing their best, and then, whilst we waited, Captain Gannington struck another match, and began to overhaul the boat we had dropped into. She was a modern, two-bowed boat, and on the stern there was painted 'Cyclone, Glasgow.' She was in pretty fair condition, and had evidently drifted into the scum and been held by it.

"Captain Gannington struck several matches, and went forrard towards the derelict. Suddenly he called to me, and I jumped over the thwarts to him. 'Look, doctor,' he said, and I saw what he meant — a mass of bones up in the bows of the boat. I stooped over them, and looked; there were the bones of at least three people, all mixed together in an extraordinary fashion, and quite clean and dry. I had a sudden thought concerning the bones, but I said nothing, for my thought was vague in some ways, and concerned the grotesque and incredible suggestion that had come to me as to the cause of that ponderous, dull thud, thud, thud thud, that beat on so infernally within the hull, and was plain to hear even now that we had got off the vessel herself. And all the while, you know, I had a sick, horrible mental picture of that frightful, wriggling mound aboard the hulk.

"As Captain Gannington struck a final match, I saw something that sickened me and the captain saw it in the same instant. The match went out, and he fumbled clumsily for another, and struck it. We saw the thing again. We had not been mistaken. A great lip of grey-white was protruding in over the edge of the boat — a great lappet of the mould was coming stealthily towards us — a live mass of *the very hull itself!* And suddenly Captain Gannington yelled out in so many words the grotesque and incredible thing I was thinking: '*She's alive!*'

"I never heard such a sound of comprehension and terror in a man's voice. The very horrified assurance of it made actual to me the thing that before had only lurked in my subconscious mind. I knew he was right;

I knew that the explanation my reason and my training both repelled and reached towards was the true one. Oh, I wonder whether anyone can possibly understand our feelings in that moment? The unmitigated horror of it and the incredibleness!

"As the light of the match burned up fully, I saw that the mass of living matter coming towards us was streaked and veined with purple, the veins standing out, enormously distended. The whole thing quivered continuously to each ponderous thud, thud, thud, thud, of that gargantuan organ that pulsed within the huge grey-white bulk. The flame of the match reached the captain's fingers, and there came to me a little sickly whiff of burned flesh, but he seemed unconscious of any pain. Then the flame went out in a brief sizzle, yet at the last moment I had seen an extraordinary raw look become visible upon the end of that monstrous, protruding lappet. It had become dewed with a hideous, purplish sweat. And with the darkness there came a sudden charnel-like stench.

"I heard the matchbox split in Captain Gannington's hands as he wrenched it open. Then he swore, in a queer frightened voice, for he had come to the end of his matches. He turned clumsily in the darkness, and tumbled over the nearest thwart, in his eagerness to get to the stern of the boat; and I after him. For we knew that thing was coming towards us through the darkness, reaching over that piteous mingled heap of human bones all jumbled together in the bows. We shouted madly to the men, and for answer saw the bows of the boat emerge dimly into view round the starboard counter of the derelict.

" 'Thank God!' I gasped out. But Captain Gannington roared to them to show a light. Yet this they could not do, for the lamp had just been stepped on in their desperate efforts to force the boat round to us.

" 'Quick! Quick!' I shouted.

" 'For God's sake, be smart, men!' roared the captain.

"And both of us faced the darkness under the port-counter, out of which we knew — but could not see — the thing was coming to us.

" 'An oar! Smart, now — pass me an oar!' shouted the captain; and reached out his hands through the gloom towards the on-coming boat. I saw a figure stand up in the bows, and hold something out to us across the intervening yards of scum. Captain Gannington swept his hands through the darkness, and encountered it.

" 'I've got it! Let go there!' he said, in a quick, tense voice.

"In the same instant the boat we were in was pressed over suddenly to starboard by some tremendous weight. Then I heard the captain shout, 'Duck y'r head, doctor!' And directly afterwards he swung the heavy, fourteen-foot oar round his head, and struck into the darkness.

There came a sudden squelch, and he struck again, with a savage grunt of fierce energy. At the second blow the boat righted with a slow movement, and directly afterwards the other boat bumped gently into ours.

"Captain Gannington dropped the oar, and, springing across to the second mate, hove him up off the thwart, and pitched him with knee and arms clear in over the bows among the men; then he shouted to me to follow, which I did, and he came after me, bringing the oar with him. We carried the second mate aft, and the captain shouted to the men to back the boat a little; then they got her bows clear of the boat we had just left, and so headed out through the scum for the open sea.

" 'Where's Tom 'Arrison?" gasped one of the men, in the midst of his exertions. He happened to be Tom Harrison's particular chum, and Captain Gannington answered him briefly enough:

" 'Dead! Pull! Don't talk!'

"Now, difficult as it had been to force the boat through the scum to our rescue, the difficulty to get clear seemed tenfold. After some five minutes pulling, the boat seemed hardly to have moved a fathom, if so much, and a quite dreadful fear took me afresh, which one of the panting men put suddenly into words, 'It's got us!' he gasped out. 'Same as poor Tom!' It was the man who had inquired where Harrison was.

" 'Shut y'r mouth an' *pull!*' roared the captain. And so another few minutes passed. Abruptly, it seemed to me that the dull, ponderous thud, thud, thud, thud came more plainly through the dark, and I stared intently over the stern. I sickened a little, for I could almost swear that the dark mass of the monster was actually *nearer* — that it was coming nearer to us through the darkness. Captain Gannington must have had the same thought, for, after a brief look into the darkness, he jumped forrard, and began to double-bank the stroke-oar.

" 'Get forrid under the oars, doctor,' he said to me rather breathlessly. 'Get in the bows, an' see if you can't free the stuff a bit round the bows.'

"I did as he told me, and a minute later I was in the bows of the boat, puddling the scum from side to side, and trying to break up the viscid, clinging muck. A heavy almost animal-like smell rose off it, and all the air seemed full of the deadening, heavy smell. I shall never find words to tell anyone on earth the whole horror of it all — the threat that seemed to hang in the very air around us, and but a little astern that incredible thing, coming, as I firmly believed, nearer, and scum holding us, like half-melted glue.

"The minutes passed in a deadly, eternal fashion, and I kept staring back astern into the darkness but never ceasing to puddle that filthy scum, striking at it and switching it from side to side until I sweated.

"Abruptly Captain Gannington sang out: 'We're gaining, lads. Pull!' And I felt the boat forge ahead perceptibly, as they gave way with renewed hope and energy. There was soon no doubt of it, for presently that hideous thud, thud, thud, thud had grown quite dim and vague somewhere astern and I could no longer see the derelict, for the night had come down tremendously dark and all the sky was thick, overset with heavy clouds. As we drew nearer and nearer to the edge of the scum, the boat moved more and more perceptibly, until suddenly we emerged with a clean, sweet, fresh sound into the open sea.

" 'Thank God!' I said aloud, and drew in the boathook, and made my way aft again to where Captain Gannington now sat once more at the tiller. I saw him looking anxiously up at the sky and across to where the lights of our vessel burned, and again he would seem to listen intently, so that I found myself listening also.

" 'What's that, Captain?' I said sharply; for it seemed to me that I heard a sound far astern, something, between a queer whine and a low whistling. 'What's that?'

" 'It's wind, doctor.' he said in a low voice. 'I wish to God we were aboard.' Then to the men: 'Pull! Put y'r backs into it, or ye'll never put y'r teeth through good bread again!' The men obeyed nobly, and we reached the vessel safely, and had the boat safely stowed before the storm came, which it did in a furious white smother out of the west. I could see it for some minutes beforehand, tearing the sea in the gloom into a wall of phosphorescent foam; and as it came nearer, that peculiar whining, piping sound grew louder and louder, until it was like a vast steam whistle rushing towards us. And when it did come, we got it very heavy indeed, so that the morning showed us nothing but a welter of white seas, with that grim derelict many a score of miles away in the smother, lost as utterly as our hearts could wish to lose her.

"When I came to examine the second mate's feet, I found them in a very extraordinary condition. The soles of them had the appearance of having been partly digested. I know of no other word that so exactly describes their condition, and the agony the man suffered must have been dreadful.

"Now," concluded the doctor, "that is what I call a case in point. If we could know exactly what the old vessel had originally been loaded with, and the juxtaposition of the various articles of her cargo, plus the heat and time she had endured, plus one or two other only guessable quantities, we should have solved the chemistry of the life-force, gentlemen. Not necessarily the *origin*, mind you; but, at least, we should have

taken a big step on the way. I've often regretted that gale, you know —
in a way, that is, in a way. It was a most amazing discovery, but at the
same time I had nothing but thankfulness to be rid of it. A most amazing
chance. I often think of the way the monster woke out of its torpor. And
that scum! The dead pigs caught in i! I fancy that was a grim kind of a
net, gentlemen. It caught many things. It —"

The old doctor sighed and nodded.

"If I could have had her bill of lading," he said, his eyes full of regret. "If — It might have told me something to help. But, anyway —"
He began to fill his pipe again. "I suppose," he ended, looking round at
us gravely, "I s'pose we humans are an ungrateful lot of beggars at the
best! But — but, what a chance? What a, chance, eh?"

# THE BAUMOFF EXPLOSIVE

DALLY, Whitlaw and I were discussing the recent stupendous explosion which had occurred in the vicinity of Berlin. We were marvelling concerning the extraordinary period of darkness that had followed, and which had aroused so much newspaper comment, with theories galore.

The papers had got hold of the fact that the War Authorities had been experimenting with a new explosive, invented by a certain chemist, named Baumoff, and they referred to it constantly as "The New Baumoff Explosive".

We were in the Club, and the fourth man at our table was John Stafford, who was professionally a medical man, but privately in the Intelligence Department. Once or twice, as we talked, I had glanced at Stafford, wishing to fire a question at him; for he had been acquainted with Baumoff. But I managed to hold my tongue; for I knew that if I asked out pointblank, Stafford (who's a good sort, but a bit of an ass as regards his almost ponderous code-of-silence) would be just as like as not to say that it was a subject upon which he felt he was not entitled to speak.

Oh, I know the old donkey's way; and when he had once said that, we might just make up our minds never to get another word out of him on the matter as long as we lived. Yet, I was satisfied to notice that he seemed a bit restless, as if he were on the itch to shove in his oar; by which I guessed that the papers we were quoting had got things very badly muddled indeed, in some way or other, at least as regarded his friend Baumoff. Suddenly, he spoke:

"What unmitigated, wicked piffle!" said Stafford, quite warm. "I tell you it is wicked, this associating of Baumoff's name with war inventions and such horrors. He was the most intensely poetical and earnest follower of the Christ that I have ever met; and it is just the brutal Irony of Circumstance that has attempted to use one of the products of his genius for a purpose of Destruction. But you'll find they won't be able to use it, in spite of their having got hold of Baumoff's formula. As an explosive it is not practicable. It is, shall I say, too impartial; there is no way of controlling it.

"I know more about it, perhaps, than any man alive; for I was Baumoff's greatest friend, and when he died, I lost the best comrade a man ever had. I need make no secret about it to you chaps. I was 'on duty' in Berlin, and I was deputed to get in touch with Baumoff. The government had long had an eye on him; he was an Experimental Chemist, you know, and altogether too jolly clever to ignore. But there was no need to worry about him. I got to know him, and we became enormous friends; for I soon found that he would never turn his abilities towards any new war-contrivance; and so, you see, I was able to enjoy my friendship with him, with a comfy conscience — a thing our chaps are not always able to do in their friendships. Oh, I tell you, it's a mean, sneaking, treacherous sort of business, ours; though it's necessary; just as some odd man, or other, has to be a hangsman. There's a number of unclean jobs to be done to keep the Social Machine running!

"I think Baumoff was the most enthusiastic intelligent believer in Christ that it will be ever possible to produce. I learned that he was compiling and evolving a treatise of most extraordinary and convincing proofs in support of the more inexplicable things concerning the life and death of Christ. He was, when I became acquainted with him, concentrating his attention particularly upon endeavouring to show that the Darkness of the Cross, between the sixth and the ninth hours, was a very real thing, possessing a tremendous significance. He intended at one sweep to smash utterly all talk of a timely thunderstorm or any of the other more or less inefficient theories which have been brought forward from time to time to explain the occurrence away as being a thing of no particular significance.

"Baumoff had a pet aversion, an atheistic Professor of Physics, named Hautch, who — using the 'marvellous' element of the life and death of Christ, as a fulcrum from which to attack Baumoff's theories — smashed at him constantly, both in his lectures and in print. Particularly did he pour bitter unbelief upon Baumoff's upholding that the Darkness of the Cross was anything more than a gloomy hour or two, magnified into blackness by the emotional inaccuracy of the Eastern mind and tongue.

"One evening, some time after our friendship had become very real, I called on Baumoff, and found him in a state of tremendous indignation over some article of the Professor's which attacked him brutally; using his theory of the Significance of the 'Darkness', as a target. Poor Baumoff! It was certainly a marvellously clever attack; the attack of a thoroughly trained, well-balanced Logician. But Baumoff was something more; he was Genius. It is a title few have any rights to; but it was his!

"He talked to me about his theory, telling me that he wanted to show me a small experiment, presently, bearing out his opinions. In his talk, he told me several things that interested me extremely. Having first reminded me of the fundamental fact that light is conveyed to the eye through the means of that indefinable medium, named the Æther. He went a step further, and pointed out to me that, from an aspect which more approached the primary, Light was a vibration of the Æther, of a certain definite number of waves per second, which possessed the power of producing upon our retina the sensation which we term Light.

"To this, I nodded; being, as of course is everyone, acquainted with so well-known a statement. From this, he took a quick, mental stride, and told me that an ineffably vague, but measurable, darkening of the atmosphere (greater or smaller according to the personality-force of the individual) was always evoked in the immediate vicinity of the human, during any period of great emotional stress.

"Step by step, Baumoff showed me how his research had led him to the conclusion that this queer darkening (a million times too subtle to be apparent to the eye) could be produced only through something which had power to disturb or temporally interrupt or break up the Vibration of Light. In other words, there was, at any time of unusual emotional activity, some disturbance of the Æther in the immediate vicinity of the person suffering, which had some effect upon the Vibration of Light, interrupting it, and producing the aforementioned infinitely vague darkening.

" 'Yes?' I said, as he paused, and looked at me, as if expecting me to have arrived at a certain definite deduction through his remarks. 'Go on.'

" 'Well,' he said, 'don't you see, the subtle darkening around the person suffering, is greater or less, according to the personality of the suffering human. Don't you?'

" 'Oh!' I said, with a little gasp of astounded comprehension, 'I see what you mean. You — you mean that if the agony of a person of ordinary personality can produce a faint disturbance of the Æther, with a consequent faint darkening, then the Agony of Christ, possessed of the Enormous Personality of the Christ, would produce a terrific disturbance of the Æther, and therefore, it might chance, of the Vibration of Light, and that this is the true explanation of the Darkness of the Cross; and that the fact of such an extraordinary and apparently unnatural and improbable Darkness having been recorded is not a thing to weaken the Marvel of Christ. But one more unutterably wonderful, infallible proof of His God-like power? Is that it? Is it? Tell me?'

"Baumoff just rocked on his chair with delight, beating one fist into the palm of his other hand, and nodding all the time to my summary. How he loved to be understood; as the Searcher always craves to be understood.

" 'And now,' he said, 'I'm going to show you something.'

"He took a tiny, corked test-tube out of his waistcoat pocket, and emptied its contents (which consisted of a single, grey-white grain, about twice the size of an ordinary pin's head) on to his dessert plate. He crushed it gently to powder with the ivory handle of a knife, then damped it gently, with a single minim of what I supposed to be water, and worked it up into a tiny patch of grey-white paste. He then took out his gold tooth-pick, and thrust it into the flame of a small chemist's spirit lamp, which had been lit since dinner as a pipe-lighter. He held the gold tooth-pick in the flame, until the narrow, gold blade glowed whitehot.

" 'Now look!' he said, and touched the end of the tooth-pick against the infinitesmal patch upon the dessert plate. There came a swift little violet flash, and suddenly I found that I was staring at Baumoff through a sort of transparent darkness, which faded swiftly into a black opaqueness. I thought at first this must be the complementary effect of the flash upon the retina. But a minute passed, and we were still in that extraordinary darkness.

" 'My Gracious! Man! What is it?' I asked, at last.

"His voice explained then, that he had produced, through the medium of chemistry, an exaggerated effect which simulated, to some extent, the disturbance in the Æther produced by waves thrown off by any person during an emotional crisis or agony. The waves, or vibrations, sent out by his experiment produced only a partial simulation of the effect he wished to show me — merely the temporary interruption of the Vibration of Light, with the resulting darkness in which we both now sat.

" 'That stuff,' said Baumoff, 'would be a tremendous explosive, under certain conditions.'

I heard him puffing at his pipe, as he spoke, but instead of the glow of the pipe shining out visible and red, there was only a faint glare that wavered and disappeared in the most extraordinary fashion.

" 'My Goodness!' I said, 'when's this going away?' And I stared across the room to where the big kerosene lamp showed only as a faintly glimmering patch in the gloom; a vague light that shivered and flashed oddly, as though I saw it through an immense gloomy depth of dark and disturbed water.

" It's all right,' Baumoff's voice said from out of the darkness. 'It's going now; in five minutes the disturbance will have quieted, and the waves of light will flow off evenly from the lamp in their normal fashion. But, whilst we're waiting, isn't it immense, eh?'

" 'Yes,' I said. 'It's wonderful; but it's rather unearthly, you know.'

" 'Oh, but I've something much finer to show you,' he said. 'The real thing. Wait another minute. The darkness is going. See! You can see the light from the lamp now quite plainly. It looks as if it were submerged in a boil of waters, doesn't it? that are growing clearer and clearer and quieter and quieter all the time.'

"It was as he said; and we watched the lamp, silently, until all signs of the disturbance of the light-carrying medium had ceased. Then Baumoff faced me once more.

" 'Now,' he said. 'You've seen the somewhat casual effects of just crude combustion of that stuff of mine. I'm going to show you the effects of combusting it in the human furnace, that is, in my own body; and then, you'll see one of the great wonders of Christ's death reproduced on a miniature scale.'

"He went across to the mantelpiece, and returned with a small, 120 minim glass and another of the tiny, corked test-tubes, containing a single grey-white grain of his chemical substance. He uncorked the test-tube, and shook the grain of substance into the minim glass, and then, with a glass stirring-rod, crushed it up in the bottom of the glass, adding water, drop by drop as he did so, until there were sixty minims in the glass.

" 'Now!' he said, and lifting it, he drank the stuff. 'We will give it thirty-five minutes,' he continued; 'then, as carbonization proceeds, you will find my pulse will increase, as also the respiration, and presently there will come the darkness again, in the subtlest, strangest fashion; but accompanied now by certain physical and psychic phenomena, which will be owing to the fact that the vibrations it will throw off, will be blent into what I might call the emotional-vibrations, which I shall give off in my distress. These will be enormously intensified, and you will possibly experience an extraordinarily interesting demonstration of the soundness of my more theoretical reasonings. I tested it by myself last week' (He waved a bandaged finger at me), 'and I read a paper to the Club on the results. They are very enthusiastic, and have promised their co-operation in the big demonstration I intend to give on next Good Friday — that's seven weeks off, to-day.'

"He had ceased smoking; but continued to talk quietly in this fashion for the next thirty-five minutes. The Club to which he had referred was a peculiar association of men, banded together under the presidentship of Baumoff himself, and having for their appellation the title of — so well as I can translate it — 'The Believers And Provers Of Christ'. If I may say so, without any thought of irreverence, they were, many of them, men fanatically crazed to uphold the Christ. You will agree later, I think, that I have not used an incorrect term, in describing the bulk of the members of this extraordinary club, which was, in its way, well worthy of one of the religio-maniacal extrudences which have been forced into temporary being by certain of the more religiously-emotional minded of our cousins across the water.

"Baumoff looked at the clock; then held out his wrist to me. 'Take my pulse,' he said, 'it's rising fast. Interesting data, you know.'

"I nodded, and drew out my watch. I had noticed that his respirations were increasing; and I found his pulse running evenly and strongly at 105. Three minutes later, it had risen to 175, and his respirations to 41. In a further three minutes, I took his pulse again, and found it running at 203, but with the rhythm regular. His respirations were then 49. He had, as I knew, excellent lungs, and his heart was sound. His lungs, I may say, were of exceptional capacity, and there was at this stage no marked dyspnoea. Three minutes later I found the pulse to be 227, and the respiration 54.

" 'You've plenty of red corpuscles, Baumoff!' I said. 'But I hope you're not going to overdo things.'

"He nodded at me, and smiled; but said nothing. Three minutes later, when I took the last pulse, it was 233, and the two sides of the heart were sending out unequal quantities of blood, with an irregular rhythm. The respiration had risen to 67 and was becoming shallow and ineffectual, and dyspnoea was becoming very marked. The small amount of arterial blood leaving the left side of the heart betrayed itself in the curious bluish and white tinge of the face.

" 'Baumoff!' I said, and began to remonstrate; but he checked me, with a queerly invincible gesture.

" 'It's all right!' he said, breathlessly, with a little note of impatience. 'I know what I'm doing all the time. You must remember I took the same degree as you in medicine.'

"It was quite true. I remembered then that he had taken his M.D. in London; and this in addition to half a dozen other degrees in different branches of the sciences in his own country. And then, even as the memory reassured me that he was not acting in ignorance of the possible danger, he called out in a curious, breathless voice:

" 'The Darkness! It's beginning. Take note of every single thing. Don't bother about me. I'm all right!'

"I glanced swiftly round the room. It was as he had said. I perceived it now. There appeared to be an extraordinary quality of gloom growing in the atmosphere of the room. A kind of bluish gloom, vague, and scarcely, as yet, affecting the transparency of the atmosphere to light.

"Suddenly, Baumoff did something that rather sickened me. He drew his wrist away from me, and reached out to a small metal box, such as one sterilizes a hypodermic in. He opened the box, and took out four rather curious looking drawing-pins, I might call them, only they had spikes of steel fully an inch long, whilst all around the rim of the heads (which were also of steel) there projected downward, parallel with the central spike, a number of shorter spikes, maybe an eighth of an inch long.

"He kicked off his pumps; then stooped and slipped his socks off, and I saw that he was wearing a pair of linen inner-socks.

" 'Antiseptic!' he said, glancing at me. 'Got my feet ready before you came. No use running unnecessary risks.' He gasped as he spoke. Then he took one of the curious little steel spikes.

" 'I've sterilized them,' he said; and therewith, with deliberation, he pressed it in up to the head into his foot between the second and third branches of the dorsal artery.

" 'For God's sake, what are you doing!' I said, half rising from my chair.

" 'Sit down!' he said, in a grim sort of voice. 'I can't have any interference. I want you simply to observe; keep note of everything. You ought to thank me for the chance, instead of worrying me, when you know I shall go my own way all the time.'

"As he spoke, he had pressed in the second of the steel spikes up to the hilt in his left instep, taking the same precaution to avoid the arteries. Not a groan had come from him; only his face betrayed the effect of this additional distress.

" 'My dear chap!' he said, observing my upsetness. 'Do be sensible. I know exactly what I'm doing. There simply must be distress, and the readiest way to reach that condition is through physical pain.' His speech had becomes a series of spasmodic words, between gasps, and sweat lay in great clear drops upon his lip and forehead. He slipped off his belt and proceeded to buckle it round both the back of his chair and his waist; as if he expected to need some support from falling.

" 'It's wicked!' I said. Baumoff made an attempt to shrug his heaving shoulders, that was, in its way, one of the most piteous things that I have seen, in its sudden laying bare of the agony that the man was making so little of.

"He was now cleaning the palms of his hands with a little sponge, which he dipped from time to time in a cup of solution. I knew what he was going to do, and suddenly he jerked out, with a painful attempt to grin, an explanation of his bandaged finger. He had held his finger in the flame of the spirit lamp, during his previous experiment; but now, as he made clear in gaspingly uttered words, he wished to simulate as far as possible the actual conditions of the great scene that he had so much in mind. He made it so clear to me that we might expect to experience something very extraordinary, that I was conscious of a sense of almost superstitious nervousness.

" 'I wish you wouldn't, Baumoff!' I said.

" 'Don't — be — silly!' he managed to say. But the two latter words were more groans than words; for between each, he had thrust home right to the heads in the palms of his hands the two remaining steel spikes. He gripped his hands shut, with a sort of spasm of savage determination, and I saw the point of one of the spikes break through the back of his hand, between the extensor tendons of the second and third fingers. A drop of blood beaded the point of the spike. I looked at Baumoff's face; and he looked back steadily at me.

" 'No interference,' he managed to ejaculate. 'I've not gone through all this for nothing. I know — what — I'm doing. Look — it's coming. Take note — everything!'

"He relapsed into silence, except for his painful gasping. I realised that I must give way, and I stared round the room, with a peculiar commingling of an almost nervous discomfort and a stirring of very real and sober curiosity.

" 'Oh,' said Baumoff, after a moment's silence, 'something's going to happen. I can tell. Oh, wait — till I — I have my — big demonstration. I'll show that brute Hautch.' ̇

"I nodded; but I doubt that he saw me; for his eyes had a distinctly in-turned look, the iris was rather relaxed. I glanced away round the room again; there was a distinct occasional breaking up of the light-rays from the lamp, giving a coming-and-going effect.

"The atmosphere of the room was also quite plainly darker — heavy, with an extraordinary sense of gloom. The bluish tint was unmistakably more in evidence; but there was, as yet, none of that opacity which we had experienced before, upon simple combustion, except for the occasional, vague coming-and-going of the lamp-light.

"Baurnoff began to speak again, getting his words out between gasps. 'Th' — this dodge of mine gets the — pain into the — the — right place. Right association of — of ideas — emotions — for — best — results. You follow me? Parallelising things — as — much as — possible. Fixing whole attention — on the — the death scene —'

"He gasped painfully for a few moments. 'We demonstrate truth of — of The Darkening; but — but there's psychic effect to be — looked for, through — results of parallelisation of — conditions. May have extraordinary simulation of — the actual thing. Keep note. Keep note.'

Then, suddenly, with a clear, spasmodic burst: 'My God, Stafford, keep note of everything. Something's going to happen. Something — wonderful — Promise not — to bother me. I know — what I'm doing.'

"Baurnoff ceased speaking, with a gasp, and there was only the labour of his breathing in the quietness of the room. As I stared at him, halting from a dozen things I needed to say, I realised suddenly that I could no longer see him quite plainly; a sort of wavering in the atmosphere, between us, made him seem momentarily unreal. The whole room had darkened perceptibly in the last thirty seconds; and as I stared around, I realised that there was a constant invisible swirl in the fast-deepening, extraordinary blue gloom that seemed now to permeate everything. When I looked at the lamp, alternate flashings of light and blue — darkness followed each other with an amazing swiftness.

" 'My God!' I heard Baumoff whispering in the half-darkness, as if to himself, 'how did Christ bear the nails!'

"I stared across at him, with an infinite discomfort, and an irritated pity troubling me; but I knew it was no use to remonstrate now. I saw him vaguely distorted through the wavering tremble of the atmosphere. It was somewhat as if I looked at him through convolutions of heated air; only there were marvellous waves of blue-blackness making gaps in my sight. Once I saw his face clearly, full of an infinite pain, that was somehow, seemingly, more spiritual than physical, and dominating everything was an expression of enormous resolution and concentration, making the livid, sweat-damp, agonized face somehow heroic and splendid.

"And then, drenching the room with waves and splashes of opaqueness, the vibration of his abnormally stimulated agony finally broke up the vibration of Light. My last, swift glance round, showed me, as it seemed, the invisible aether boiling and eddying in a tremendous fashion; and, abruptly, the flame of the lamp was lost in an extraordinary swirling patch of light, that marked its position for several moments, shimmering and deadening, shimmering and deadening; until, abruptly, I saw neither that glimmering patch of light, nor anything else. I was suddenly lost in a black opaqueness of night, through which came the fierce, painful breathing of Baumoff.

"A full minute passed; but so slowly that, if I had not been counting Baumoff's respirations, I should have said that it was five. Then Baumoff spoke suddenly, in a voice that was, somehow, curiously changed — a certain toneless note in it:

" 'My God!' he said, from out of the darkness, 'what must Christ have suffered!'

"It was in the succeeding silence, that I had the first realisation that I was vaguely afraid; but the feeling was too indefinite and unfounded, and I might say subconscious, for me to face it out. Three minutes passed, whilst I counted the almost desperate respirations that came to me through the darkness. Then Baumoff began to speak again, and still in that peculiarly altering voice:

" 'By Thy Agony and Bloody Sweat,' he muttered. Twice he repeated this. It was plain indeed that he had fixed his whole attention with tremendous intensity, in his abnormal state, upon the death scene.

"The effect upon me of his intensity was interesting and in some ways extraordinary. As well as I could, I analysed my sensations and emotions and general state of mind, and realised that Baumoff was producing an effect upon me that was almost hypnotic.

"Once, partly because I wished to get my level by the aid of a normal remark, and also because I was suddenly newly anxious by a change in the breathsounds, I asked Baumoff how he was. My voice going with a peculiar and really uncomfortable blankness through that impenetrable blackness of opacity.

"He said: 'Hush! I'm carrying the Cross.' And, do you know, the effect of those simple words, spoken in that new, toneless voice, in that atmosphere of almost unbearable tenseness, was so powerful that, suddenly, with eyes wide open, I saw Baumoff clear and vivid against that unnatural darkness, carrying a Cross. Not, as the picture is usually shown of the Christ, with it crooked over the shoulder; but with the Cross gripped just under the cross-piece in his arms, and the end trailing behind, along rocky ground. I saw even the pattern of the grain of the rough wood, where some of the bark had been ripped away; and under the trailing end there was a tussock of tough wire-grass, that had been uprooted by the lowing end, and dragged and ground along upon the rocks, between the end of the Cross and the rocky ground. I can see the thing now, as I speak. Its vividness was extraordinary; but it had come and gone like a flash, and I was sitting there in the darkness, mechanically counting the respirations; yet unaware that I counted.

"As I sat there, it came to me suddenly — the whole entire marvel of the thing that Baumoff had achieved. I was sitting there in a darkness which was an actual reproduction of the miracle of the Darkness of the Cross. In short, Baumoff had, by producing in himself an abnormal condition, developed an Energy of Emotion that must have almost, in its effects, paralleled the Agony of the Cross. And in so doing, he had shown from an entirely new and wonderful point, the indisputable truth of the stupendous personality and the enormous spiritual force of the

Christ. He had evolved and made practical to the average understanding a proof that would make to live again the reality of that wonder of the world — *Christ*. And for all this, I had nothing but admiration of an almost stupefied kind.

"But, at this point, I felt that the experiment should stop. I had a strangely nervous craving for Baumoff to end it right there and then, and not to try to parallel the psychic conditions. I had, even then, by some queer aid of sub-conscious suggestion, a vague reaching-out-towards the danger of "monstrosity" being induced, instead of any actual knowledge gained.

" 'Baumoff!' I said. 'Stop it.' "

"But he made no reply, and for some minutes there followed a silence, that was unbroken, save by his gasping breathing. Abruptly, Baumoff said, between his gasps: 'Woman — behold — thy — son.' He muttered this several times, in the same uncomfortably toneless voice in which he had spoken since the darkness became complete.

" 'Baumoff.' I said again. 'Baumoff! Stop it.' " And as I listened for his answer, I was relieved to think that his breathing was less shallow. The abnormal demand for oxygen was evidently being met, and the extravagant call upon the heart's efficiency was being relaxed.

" 'Baumoff!' I said, once more. 'Baumoff! Stop it!' "

"And, as I spoke, abruptly, I thought the room was shaken a little.

"Now, I had already as you will have realised, been vaguely conscious of a peculiar and growing nervousness. I think that is the word that best describes it, up to this moment. At this curious little shake that seemed to stir through the utterly dark room, I was suddenly more than nervous. I felt a thrill of actual and literal fear; yet with no sufficient cause of reason to justify me; so that, after sitting very tense for some long minutes, and feeling nothing further, I decided that I needed to take myself in hand, and keep a firmer grip upon my nerves. And then, just as I had arrived at this more comfortable state of mind, the room was shaken again, with the most curious and sickening oscillatory movement, that was beyond all comfort of denial.

" 'My God!' I whispered. And then, with a sudden effort of courage, I called: 'Baumoff! For God's sake stop it."

"You've no idea of the effort it took to speak aloud into that darkness; and when I did speak, the sound of my voice set me afresh on edge. It went so empty and raw across the room; and somehow, the room seemed to be incredibly big. Oh, I wonder whether you realise how beastly I felt, without my having to make any further effort to tell you.

"And Baumoff never answered a word; but I could hear him breathing, a little fuller; though still heaving his thorax painfully, in his need for air. The incredible shaking of the room eased away; and there succeeded a spasm of quiet, in which I felt that it was my duty to get up and step across to Baumoffs chair. But I could not do it. Somehow, I would not have touched Baumoff then for any cause whatever. Yet, even in that moment, as now I know, I was not aware that I was afraid to touch Baumoff.

"And then the oscillations commenced again. I felt the seat of my trousers slide against the seat of my chair, and I thrust out my legs, spreading my feet against the carpet, to keep me from sliding off one way or the other on to the floor. To say I was afraid, was not to describe my state at all. I was terrified. And suddenly, I had comfort, in the most extraordinary fashion; for a single idea literally glazed into my brain, and gave me a reason to which to cling. It was a single line:

" 'Æther, the soul of iron and sundry stuffs' which Baumoff had once taken as a text for an extraordinary lecture on vibrations, in the earlier days of our friendship. He had formulated the suggestion that, in embryo, Matter was, from a primary aspect, a localised vibration, traversing a closed orbit. These primary localised vibrations were inconceivably minute. But were capable, under certain conditions, of combining under the action of keynote-vibrations into secondary vibrations of a size and shape to be determined by a multitude of only guessable factors. These would sustain their new form, so long as nothing occurred to disorganise their combination or depreciate or divert their energy — their unity being partially determined by the inertia of the still Æther outside of the closed path which their area of activities covered. And such combination of the primary localised vibrations was neither more nor less than matter. Men and worlds, aye! and universes.

"And then he had said the thing that struck me most. He had said, that if it were possible to produce a vibration of the Æther of a sufficient energy, it would be possible to disorganise or confuse the vibration of matter. That, given a machine capable of creating a vibration of the Æther of a sufficient energy, he would engage to destroy not merely the world, but the whole universe itself, including heaven and hell themselves, if such places existed, and had such existence in a material form.

"I remember how I looked at him, bewildered by the pregnancy and scope of his imagination. And now his lecture had come back to me to help my courage with the sanity of reason. Was it not possible that the Æther disturbance which he had produced, had sufficient energy to cause some disorganisation of the vibration of matter, in the immediate vicinity, and had thus created a miniature quaking of the ground all about the house, and so set the house gently a-shake?

"And then, as this thought came to me, another and a greater, flashed into my mind. 'My God!' I said out loud into the darkness of the room. It explains one more mystery of the Cross, the disturbance of the Æther caused by Christ's Agony, disorganised the vibration of matter in the vicinity of the Cross, and there was then a small local earthquake, which opened the graves, and rent the veil, possibly by disturbing its supports. And, of course, the earthquake was an effect, and not a cause, as belittlers of the Christ have always insisted.

" 'Baumoff!' I called. 'Baumoff, you've proved another thing. Baumoff! Baumoff! Answer me. Are you all right?'

"Baumoff answered, sharp and sudden out of the darkness; but not to me:

" 'My God!' he said. 'My God!' His voice came out at me, a cry of veritable mental agony. He was suffering, in some hypnotic, induced fashion, something of the very agony of the Christ Himself.

" 'Baumoff!" I shouted, and forced myself to my feet. I heard his chair clattering, as he sat there and shook. 'Baumoff!'

An extraordinary quake went across the floor of the room, and I heard a creaking of the woodwork, and something fell and smashed in the darkness. Baumoffs gasps hurt me; but I stood there. I dared not go to him. I knew then that I was afraid of him — of his condition, or something I don't know what. But, oh, I was horribly afraid of him.

" 'Bau —' I began, but suddenly I was afraid even to speak to him. And I could not move. Abruptly, he cried out in a tone of incredible anguish:

" 'Eloi, Eloi, lama sabachthani!'But the last word changed in his mouth, from his dreadful hypnotic grief and pain, to a scream of simply infernal terror.

"And, suddenly, a horrible mocking voice roared out in the room, from Baumoff's chair: 'Eloi, Eloi, lama sabachthani!'

"Do you understand, the voice was not Baumoff's at all. It was not a voice of despair; but a voice sneering in an incredible, bestial, monstrous fashion. In the succeeding silence, as I stood in an ice of fear, I knew that Baumoff no longer gasped. The room was absolutely silent, the most dreadful and silent place in all this world. Then I bolted; caught my foot, probably in the invisible edge of the hearth-rug, and pitched headlong into a blaze of internal brain-stars. After which, for a very long time, certainly some hours, I knew nothing of any kind.

"I came back into this Present, with a dreadful headache oppressing me, to the exclusion of all else. But the Darkness had dissipated. I rolled over on to my side, and saw Baumoffand forgot even the pain in my head. He was leaning forward towards me: his eyes wide open, but dull. His face was enormously swollen, and there was, somehow, something beastly about him. He was dead, and the belt about him and the chair-back, alone prevented him from falling forward on to me. His tongue was thrust out of one corner of his mouth. I shall always remember how he looked. He was leering, like a human-beast, more than a man.

"I edged away from him, across the floor; but I never stopped looking at him, until I had got to the other side of the door, and closed between us. Of course, I got my balance in a bit, and went back to him; but there was nothing I could do.

"Baumoff died of heart-failure, of course, obviously! I should never be so foolish as to suggest to any sane jury that, in his extraordinary, self-hypnotised, defenseless condition, he was "entered" by some Christ-apeing Monster of the Void. I've too much respect for my own claim to be a common-sensible man, to put forward such an idea with seriousness! Oh, I know I may seem to speak with a jeer; but what can I do but jeer at myself and all the world, when I dare not acknowledge, even secretly to myself, what my own thoughts are. Baumoff did, undoubtedly die of heart-failure; and, for the rest, how much was I hypnotised into believing. Only, there was over by the far wall, where it had been shaken down to the floor from a solidly fastened-up bracket, a little pile of glass that had once formed a piece of beautiful Venetian glassware. You remember that I heard something fall, when the room shook. Surely the room did shake? Oh, I must stop thinking. My head goes round.

"The explosive the papers are talking about. Yes, that's Baumoff's; that makes it all seem true, doesn't it? They had the darkness at Berlin, after the explosion. There is no getting away from that. The Government know only that Baumoff's formulae is capable of producing the largest quantity of gas, in the shortest possible time. That, in short, it is ideally explosive. So it is; but I imagine it will prove an explosive, as I have already said, and as experience has proved, a little too impartial in its action for it to create enthusiasm on either side of a battlefield. Perhaps this is but a mercy, in disguise; certainly a mercy, if Baumoff's theories as to the possibility of disorganising matter, be anywhere near to the truth.

"I have thought sometimes that there might be a more normal explanation of the dreadful thing that happened at the end. Baumoff may have ruptured a blood-vessel in the brain, owing to the enormous arterial pressure that his experiment induced; and the voice I heard and the mockery and the horrible expression and leer may have been nothing more than the immediate outburst and expression of the natural "obliqueness" of a deranged mind, which so often turns up a side of a man's nature and produces an inversion of character, that is the very complement of his normal state. And certainly, poor Baumoff's normal religious attitude was one of marvellous reverence and loyalty towards the Christ.

"Also, in support of this line of explanation, I have frequently observed that the voice of a person suffering from mental derangement is frequently wonderfully changed, and has in it often a very repellant and inhuman quality. I try to think that this explanation fits the case. But I can never forget that room. Never."

# A TROPICAL HORROR

WE are a hundred and thirty days out from Melbourne, and for three weeks we have lain in this sweltering calm.

It is midnight, and our watch on deck until four a.m. I go out and sit on the hatch. A minute later, Joky, our youngest 'prentice, joins me for a chatter. Many are the hours we have sat thus and talked in the night watches; though, to be sure, it is Joky who does the talking. I am content to smoke and listen, giving an occasional grunt at seasons to show that I am attentive.

Joky has been silent for some time, his head bent in meditation. Suddenly he looks up, evidently with the intention of making some remark. As he does so, I see his face stiffen with a nameless horror. He crouches back, his eyes staring past me at some unseen fear. Then his mouth opens. He gives forth a strangulated cry and topples backward off the hatch, striking his head against the deck. Fearing I know not what, I turn to look.

Great Heavens! Rising above the bulwarks, seen plainly in the bright moonlight, is a vast slobbering mouth a fathom across. From the huge dripping lips hang great tentacles. As I look the Thing comes further over the rail. It is rising, rising, higher and higher. There are no eyes visible; only that fearful slobbering mouth set on the tremendous trunk-like neck; which, even as I watch, is curling inboard with the stealthy celerity of an enormous eel. Over it comes in vast heaving folds. Will it never end? The ship gives a slow, sullen roll to starboard as she feels the weight. Then the tail, a broad, flat-shaped mass, slips over the teak rail and falls with a loud slump on to the deck.

For a few seconds the hideous creature lies heaped in writhing, slimy coils. Then, with quick, darting movements, the monstrous head travels along the deck. Close by the mainmast stand the harness casks, and alongside of these a freshly opened cask of salt beef with the top loosely replaced. The smell of the meat seems to attract the monster, and I can hear it sniffing with a vast indrawing breath. Then those lips open, displaying four huge fangs; there is a quick forward motion of the head, a sudden crashing, crunching sound, and beef and barrel have disappeared. The noise brings one of the ordinary seamen out of the fo'cas'le. Coming into the night, he can see nothing for a moment. Then, as he gets further aft, he sees, and with horrified cries rushes forward. Too late! From the mouth of the Thing there flashes forth a long, broad blade of glistening white, set with fierce teeth. I avert my eyes, but cannot shut out the sickening "Glut! Glut!" that follows.

The man on the "look-out," attracted by the disturbance, has witnessed the tragedy, and flies for refuge into the fo'cas'le, flinging to the heavy iron door after him.

The carpenter and sailmaker come running out from the half-deck in their drawers. Seeing the awful Thing, they rush aft to the cabin with shouts of fear. The second mate, after one glance over the break of the poop, runs down the companion-way with the helmsman after him. I can hear them barring the scuttle, and abruptly I realise that I am on the main deck alone.

So far I have forgotten my own danger. The past few minutes seem like a portion of an awful dream. Now, however, I comprehend my position and, shaking off the horror that has held me, turn to seek safety. As I do so my eyes fall upon Joky, lying huddled and senseless with fright where he has fallen. I cannot leave him there. Close by stands the empty half-deck — a little steel-built house with iron doors. The lee one is hooked open. Once inside I am safe.

Up to the present the Thing has seemed to be unconscious of my presence. Now, however, the huge barrel-like head sways in my direction; then comes a muffled bellow, and the great tongue flickers in and out as the brute turns and swirls aft to meet me. I know there is not a moment to lose, and, picking up the helpless lad, I make a run for the open door. It is only distant a few yards, but that awful shape is coming down the deck to me in great wreathing coils. I reach the house and tumble in with my burden; then out on deck again to unhook and close the door. Even as I do so something white curls round the end of the house. With a bound I am inside and the door is shut and bolted. Through the thick glass of the ports I see the Thing sweep round the house, in vain search for me.

Joky has not moved yet; so, kneeling down, I loosen his shirt collar and sprinkle some water from the breaker over his face. While I am doing this I hear Morgan shout something; then comes a great shriek of terror, and again that sickening "Glut! Glut!"

Joky stirs uneasily, rubs his eyes, and sits up suddenly.

"Was that Morgan shouting —?" He breaks off with a cry. "Where are we? I have had such awful dreams!"

At this instant there is a sound of running footsteps on the deck and I hear Morgan's voice at the door.

"Tom, open —!"

He stops abruptly and gives an awful cry of despair. Then I hear him rush forward. Through the porthole, I see him spring into the fore rigging and scramble madly aloft. Something steals up after him. It shows white in the moonlight. It wraps itself around his right ankle. Morgan stops dead, plucks out his sheath-knife, and hacks fiercely at the fiendish thing. It lets go, and in a second he is over the top and running for dear life up the t'gallant rigging.

A time of quietness follows, and presently I see that the day is breaking. Not a sound can be heard save the heavy gasping breathing of the Thing. As the sun rises higher the creature stretches itself out along the deck and seems to enjoy the warmth. Still no sound, either from the men forward or the officers aft. I can only suppose that they are afraid of attracting its attention. Yet, a little later, I hear the report of a pistol away aft, and looking out I see the serpent raise its huge head as though listening. As it does so I get a good view of the fore part, and in the daylight see what the night has hidden.

There, right about the mouth, is a pair of little pig-eyes, that seem to twinkle with a diabolical intelligence. It is swaying its head slowly from side to side; then, without warning, it turns quickly and looks right in through the port. I dodge out of sight; but not soon enough. It has seen me, and brings its great mouth up against the glass.

I hold my breath. My God! If it breaks the glass! I cower, horrified. From the direction of the port there comes a loud, harsh, scraping sound. I shiver. Then I remember that there are little iron doors to shut over the ports in bad weather. Without a moment's waste of time I rise to my feet and slam to the door over the port. Then I go round to the others and do the same. We are now in darkness, and I tell Joky in a whisper to light the lamp, which, after some fumbling, he does.

About an hour before midnight I fall asleep. I am awakened suddenly some hours later by a scream of agony and the rattle of a water-dipper. There is a slight scuffling sound; then that soul-revolting "Glut! Glut!"

I guess what has happened. One of the men forrad has slipped out of the fo'cas'le to try and get a little water. Evidently he has trusted to the darkness to hide his movements. Poor beggar! He has paid for his attempt with his life!

After this I cannot sleep, though the rest of the night passes quietly enough. Towards morning I doze a bit, but wake every few minutes with a start. Joky is sleeping peacefully; indeed, he seems worn out with the terrible strain of the past twenty-four hours. About eight a.m. I call him, and we make a light breakfast off the dry ship's biscuit and water. Of the latter happily we have a good supply. Joky seems more himself, and starts to talk a little — possibly somewhat louder than is safe; for, as he chatters on, wondering how it will end, there comes a tremendous blow against the side of the house, making it ring again. After this Joky is very silent. As we sit there I cannot but wonder what all the rest are doing, and how the poor beggars forrad are faring, cooped up without water, as the tragedy of the night has proved.

Towards noon, I hear a loud bang, followed by a terrific bellowing. Then comes a great smashing of woodwork, and the cries of men in pain. Vainly I ask myself what has happened. I begin to reason. By the sound of the report it was evidently something much heavier than a rifle or pistol, and judging from the mad roaring of the Thing, the shot must have done some execution. On thinking it over further, I become convinced that, by some means, those aft have got hold of the small signal cannon we carry, and though I know that some have been hurt, perhaps killed, yet a feeling of exultation seizes me as I listen to the roars of the Thing, and realise that it is badly wounded, perhaps mortally. After a while, however, the bellowing dies away, and only an occasional roar, denoting more of anger than aught else, is heard.

Presently I become aware, by the ship's canting over to starboard, that the creature has gone over to that side, and a great hope springs up within me that possibly it has had enough of us and is going over the rail into the sea. For a time all is silent and my hope grows stronger. I lean across and nudge Joky, who is sleeping with his head on the table. He starts up sharply with a loud cry.

"Hush!" I whisper hoarsely. "I'm not certain, but I do believe it's gone."

Joky's face brightens wonderfully, and he questions me eagerly. We wait another hour or so, with hope ever rising. Our confidence is returning fast. Not a sound can we hear, not even the breathing of the Beast. I get out some biscuits, and Joky, after rummaging in the locker, produces a small piece of pork and a bottle of ship's vinegar. We fall to with a relish. After our long abstinence from food the meal acts on us like wine, and what must Joky do but insist on opening the door, to make sure the Thing has gone. This I will not allow, telling him that at least it will be safer to open the iron port-covers first and have a look out. Joky argues, but I am immovable. He becomes excited. I believe the youngster is lightheaded. Then, as I turn to unscrew one of the after-covers, Joky makes a dash at the door. Before he can undo the bolts I have him, and after a short struggle lead him back to the table. Even as I endeavour to quieten him there comes at the starboard door — the door that Joky has tried to open — a sharp, loud sniff, sniff, followed immediately by a thunderous grunting howl and a foul stench of putrid breath sweeps in under the door. A great trembling takes me, and were it not for the carpenter's tool-chest I should fall. Joky turns very white and is violently sick, after which he is seized by a hopeless fit of sobbing.

Hour after hour passes, and, weary to death, I lie down on the chest upon which I have been sitting, and try to rest.

It must be about half-past two in the morning, after a somewhat longer doze, that I am suddenly awakened by a most tremendous uproar away forrad — men's voices shrieking, cursing, praying; but in spite of the terror expressed, so weak and feeble; while in the midst, and at times broken off short with that hellishly suggestive "Glut! Glut!" is the unearthly bellowing of the Thing. Fear incarnate seizes me, and I can only fall on my knees and pray. Too well I know what is happening.

Joky has slept through it all, and I am thankful.

Presently, under the door there steals a narrow ribbon of light, and I know that the day has broken on the second morning of our imprisonment. I let Joky sleep on. I will let him have peace while he may. Time passes, but I take little notice. The Thing is quiet, probably sleeping. About midday I eat a little biscuit and drink some of the water. Joky still sleeps. It is best so.

A sound breaks the stillness. The ship gives a slight heave, and I know that once more the Thing is awake. Round the deck it moves, causing the ship to roll perceptibly. Once it goes forrad — I fancy to again explore the fo'cas'le. Evidently it finds nothing, for it returns almost immediately. It pauses a moment at the house, then goes on further aft. Up aloft, somewhere in the fore-rigging, there rings out a peal of wild laughter, though sounding very faint and far away. The Horror stops suddenly. I listen intently, but hear nothing save a sharp creaking beyond the after end of the house, as though a strain had come upon the rigging.

A minute later I hear a cry aloft, followed almost instantly by a loud crash on deck that seems to shake the ship. I wait in anxious fear. What is happening? The minutes pass slowly. Then comes another frightened shout. It ceases suddenly. The suspense has become terrible, and I am no longer able to bear it. Very cautiously I open one of the after port-covers, and peep out to see a fearful sight. There, with its tail upon the deck and its vast body curled round the mainmast, is the monster, its head above the topsail yard, and its great claw-armed tentacle waving in the air. It is the first proper sight that I have had of the Thing. Good Heavens! It must weigh a hundred tons! Knowing that I shall have time, I open the port itself, then crane my head out and look up. There on the extreme end of the lower topsail yard I see one of the able seamen. Even down here I note the staring horror of his face. At this moment he sees me and gives a weak, hoarse cry for help. I can do nothing for him. As I look the great tongue shoots out and licks him off the yard, much as might a dog a fly off the window-pane.

Higher still, but happily out of reach, are two more of the men. As far as I can judge they are lashed to the mast above the royal yard. The Thing attempts to reach them, but after a futile effort it ceases, and starts to slide down, coil on coil, to the deck. While doing this I notice a great gaping wound on its body some twenty feet above the tail.

I drop my gaze from aloft and look aft. The cabin door is torn from its hinges, and the bulkhead — which, unlike the half-deck, is of teak wood — is partly broken down. With a shudder I realise the cause of those cries after the cannon-shot. Turning I screw my head round and try to see the foremast, but cannot. The sun, I notice, is low, and the night is near. Then I draw in my head and fasten up both port and cover.

How will it end? Oh! how will it end?

After a while Joky wakes up. He is very restless, yet though he has eaten nothing during the day I cannot get him to touch anything.

Night draws on. We are too weary — too dispirited to talk. I lie down, but not to sleep. . . . Time passes.

* * * *

A ventilator rattles violently somewhere on the main deck, and there sounds constantly that slurring, gritty noise. Later I hear a cat's agonised howl, and then again all is quiet. Some time after comes a great splash alongside. Then, for some hours all is silent as the grave. Occasionally I sit up on the chest and listen, yet never a whisper of noise comes to me. There is an absolute silence, even the monotonous creak of the gear has died away entirely, and at last a real hope is springing up within me. That splash, this silence — surely I am justified in hoping. I do not wake Joky this time. I will prove first for myself that all is safe. Still I wait. I will run no unnecessary risks. After a time I creep to the after-port and will listen; but there is no sound. I put up my hand and feel at the screw, then again I hesitate, yet not for long. Noiselessly I begin to unscrew the fastening of the heavy shield. It swings loose on its hinge, and I pull it back and peer out. My heart is beating madly. Everything seems strangely dark outside. Perhaps the moon has gone behind a cloud. Suddenly a beam of moonlight enters through the port, and goes as quickly. I stare out. Something moves. Again the light streams in, and now I seem to be looking into a great cavern, at the bottom of which quivers and curls something palely white.

My heart seems to stand still! It is the Horror! I start back and seize the iron port-flap to slam it to. As I do so, something strikes the glass like a steam ram, shatters it to atoms, and flicks past me into the berth. I scream and spring away. The port is quite filled with it. The lamp shows it dimly. It is curling and twisting here and there. It is as thick as a tree, and covered with a smooth slimy skin. At the end is a great claw, like a lobster's, only a thousand times larger. I cower down into the farthest corner. . . . It has broken the tool-chest to pieces with one click of those frightful mandibles. Joky has crawled under a bunk. The Thing sweeps round in my direction. I feel a drop of sweat trickle slowly down my face — it tastes salty. Nearer comes that awful death. . . . *Crash!* I roll over backwards. It has crushed the water breaker against which I leant, and I am rolling in the water across the floor. The claw drives up, then down, with a quick uncertain movement, striking the deck a dull, heavy blow, a foot from my head. Joky gives a little gasp of horror. Slowly the Thing rises and starts feeling its way round the berth. It plunges into a bunk and pulls out a bolster, nips it in half and drops it, then moves on. It is feeling along the deck. As it does so it comes across a half of the bolster. It seems to toy with it, then picks it up and takes it out through the port. . . .

A wave of putrid air fills the berth. There is a grating sound, and something enters the port again — something white and tapering and set with teeth. Hither and thither it curls, rasping over the bunks, ceiling, and deck, with a noise like that of a great saw at work. Twice it flickers above my head, and I close my eyes. Then off it goes again. It sounds now on the opposite side of the berth and nearer to Joky. Suddenly the harsh, raspy noise becomes muffled, as though the teeth were passing across some soft substance. Joky gives a horrid little scream, that breaks off into a bubbling, whistling sound. I open my eyes. The tip of the vast tongue is curled tightly round something that drips, then is quickly withdrawn, allowing the moonbeams to steal again into the berth. I rise to my feet. Looking round, I note in a mechanical sort of way the wrecked state of the berth — the shattered chests, dismantled bunks, and something else —

"Joky!" I cry, and tingle all over.

There is that awful Thing again at the port. I glance round for a weapon. I will revenge Joky. Ah! there, right under the lamp, where the wreck of the carpenter's chest strews the floor, lies a small hatchet. I spring forward and seize it. It is small, but so keen — so keen! I feel its razor edge lovingly. Then I am back at the port. I stand to one side and raise my weapon. The great tongue is feeling its way to those fearsome remains. It reaches them. As it does so, with a scream of "Joky! Joky!" I strike savagely again and again and again, gasping as I strike; once more, and the monstrous mass falls to the deck, writhing like a hideous eel. A vast, warm flood rushes in through the porthole. There is a sound of breaking steel and an enormous bellowing. A singing comes in my ears and grows louder — louder. Then the berth grows indistinct and suddenly dark.

*Extract from the log of the steamship Hispaniola.*

June 24. — Lat. — N. Long. — W. 11 a.m. — Sighted four-masted barque about four points on the port bow, flying signal of distress. Ran down to her and sent a boat aboard. She proved to be the Glen Doon, homeward bound from Melbourne to London. Found things in a terrible state. Decks covered with blood and slime. Steel deck-house stove in. Broke open door, and discovered youth of about nineteen in last stage of inanition, also part remains of boy about fourteen years of age. There was a great quantity of blood in the place, and a huge curled-up mass of whitish flesh, weighing about half a ton, one end of which appeared to have been hacked through with a sharp instrument. Found forecastle door open and hanging from one hinge. Doorway bulged, as though something had been forced through. Went inside. Terrible state of affairs, blood everywhere, broken chests, smashed bunks, but no men nor remains. Went aft again and found youth showing signs of recovery. When he came round, gave the name of Thompson. Said they had been attacked by a huge serpent — thought it must have been sea-serpent. He was too weak to say much, but told us there were some men up the mainmast. Sent a hand aloft, who reported them lashed to the royal mast, and quite dead. Went aft to the cabin. Here we found the bulkhead smashed to pieces, and the cabin-door lying on the deck near the after-hatch. Found body of captain down lazarette, but no officers. Noticed amongst the wreckage part of the carriage of a small cannon. Came aboard again.

Have sent the second mate with six men to work her into port. Thompson is with us. He has written out his version of the affair. We certainly consider that the state of the ship, as we found her, bears out in every respect his story.

(Signed)
William Norton (Master).
Tom Briggs (1st Mate).

# DEMONS OF THE SEA

"COME OUT on deck and have a look, Darky!" Jepson cried, rushing into the half deck. "The Old Man says there's been a submarine earthquake, and the sea's all bubbling and muddy!"

Obeying the summons of Jepson's excited tone, I followed him out. It was as he had said; the everlasting blue of the ocean was mottled with splotches of a muddy hue, and at times a large bubble would appear, to burst with a loud "pop." Aft, the skipper and the three mates could be seen on the poop, peering at the sea through their glasses. As I gazed out over the gently heaving water, far off to windward something was hove up into the evening air. It appeared to be a mass of seaweed, but fell back into the water with a sullen plunge as though it were something more substantial. Immediately after this strange occurrence, the sun set with tropical swiftness, and in the brief afterglow things assumed a strange unreality.

The crew were all below, no one but the mate and the helmsman remaining on the poop. Away forward, on the topgallant forecastle head the dim figure of the man on lookout could be seen, leaning against the forestay. No sound was heard save the occasional jingle of a chain sheet, of the flog of the steering gear as a small swell passed under our counter. Presently the mate's voice broke the silence, and, looking up, I saw that the Old Man had come on deck, and was talking with him. From the few stray words that could be overheard, I knew they were talking of the strange happenings of the day.

Shortly after sunset, the wind, which had been fresh during the day, died down, and with its passing the air grew oppressively hot. Not long after two bells, the mate sung out for me, and ordered me to fill a bucket from overside and bring it to him. When I had carried out his instructions, he placed a thermometer in the bucket.

"Just as I thought," he muttered, removing the instrument and showing it to the skipper; "ninety-nine degrees. Why, the sea's hot enough to make tea with!"

"Hope it doesn't get any hotter," growled the latter; "if it does, we shall all be boiled alive."

At a sign from the mate, I emptied the bucket and replaced it in the rack, after which I resumed my former position by the rail. The Old Man and the mate walked the poop side by side. The air grew hotter as the hours passed and after a long period of silence broken only by the occasional "pop" of a bursting gas bubble, the moon arose. It shed but a feeble light, however, as a heavy mist had arisen from the sea, and through this, the moonbeams struggled weakly. The mist, we decided, was due to the excessive heat of the sea water; it was a very wet mist, and we were soon soaked to the skin. Slowly the interminable night wore on, and the sun arose, looking dim and ghostly through the mist that rolled and billowed about the ship. From time to time we took the temperature of the sea, although we found but a slight increase therein. No work was done, and a feeling as of something impending pervaded the ship.

The fog horn was kept going constantly, as the lookout peered through the wreathing mists. The captain walked the poop in company with the mates, and once the third mate spoke and pointed out into the clouds of fog. All eyes followed his gesture; we saw what was apparently a black line, which seemed to cut the whiteness of the billows. It reminded us of nothing so much as an enormous cobra standing on its tail. As we looked it vanished. The grouped mates were evidently puzzled; there seemed to be a difference of opinion among them. Presently as they argued, I heard the second mate's voice:

"That's all rot," he said. "I've seen things in fog before, but they've always turned out to be imaginary."

The third shook his head and made some reply I could not overhear, but no further comment was made. Going below that afternoon, I got a short sleep, and on coming on deck at eight bells, I found that the steam still held us; if anything, it seemed to be thicker than ever. Hansard, who had been taking the temperatures during my watch below, informed me that the sea was three degrees hotter, and that the Old Man was getting into a rare old state. At three bells I went forward to have a look over the bows, and a chin with Stevenson, whose lookout it was. On gaining the forecastle head, I went to the side and looked down into the water. Stevenson came over and stood beside me.

"Rum go, this," he grumbled.

He stood by my side for a time in silence; we seemed to be hypnotized by the gleaming surface of the sea. Suddenly out of the depths, right before us, there arose a monstrous black face. It was like a frightful caricature of a human countenance. For a moment we gazed petrified; my blood seemed to suddenly turn to ice water; I was unable to move. With a mighty effort of will, I regained my self-control and, grasping Stevenson's arm, I found I could do no more than croak, my powers of speech seemed gone. "Look!" I gasped. "Look!"

Stevenson continued to stare into the sea, like a man turned to stone. He seemed to stoop further over, as if to examine the thing more closely.

"Lord," he exclaimed, "it must be the devil himself!"

As though the sound of his voice had broken a spell, the thing disappeared. My companion looked at me, while I rubbed my eyes, thinking that I had been asleep, and that the awful vision had been a frightful nightmare. One look at my friend, however, disabused me of any such thought. His face wore a puzzled expression.

"Better go aft and tell the Old Man," he faltered.

I nodded and left the forecastle head, making my way aft like one in a trance. The skipper and the mate were standing at the break of the poop, and running up the ladder I told them what we had seen.

"Bosh!" sneered the Old Man. "You've been looking at your own ugly reflection in the water."

Nevertheless, in spite of his ridicule, he questioned me closely. Finally he ordered the mate forward to see it he could see anything. The latter, however, returned in a few moments, to report that nothing unusual could be seen. Four bells were struck, and we were relieved for tea. Coming on deck afterward, I found the men clustered together forward. The sole topic of conversation with them was the thing that Stevenson and I had seen.

"I suppose, Darky, it couldn't have been a reflection by any chance, could it?" one of the older men asked.

"Ask Stevenson," I replied as I made my way aft.

At eight bells, my watch came on deck again, to find that nothing further had developed. But, about an hour before midnight, the mate, thinking to have a smoke, sent me to his room for a box of matches with which to light his pipe. It took me no time to clatter down the brass-treaded ladder, and back to the poop, where I handed him the desired article. Taking the box, he removed a match and struck it on the heel of his boot. As he did so, far out in the night a muffled screaming arose. Then came a clamor as of hoarse braying, like an ass but considerably deeper, and with a horribly suggestive human note running through it.

"Good God! Did you hear that, Darky?" asked the mate in awed tones.

"Yes, sir," I replied, listening — and scarcely noticing his question — for a repetition of the strange sounds. Suddenly the frightful bellowing broke out afresh. The mate's pipe fell to the deck with a clatter.

"Run for'ard!" he cried. "Quick, now, and see if you can see anything."

With my heart in my mouth, and pulses pounding madly I raced forward. The watch were all up on the forecastle head, clustered around the lookout. Each man was talking and gesticulating wildly. They became silent, and turned questioning glances toward me as I shouldered my way among them.

"Have you seen anything?" I cried.

Before I could receive an answer, a repetition of the horrid sounds broke out again, profaning the night with their horror. They seemed to have definite direction now, in spite of the fog that enveloped us. Undoubtedly, too, they were nearer. Pausing a moment to make sure of their bearing, I hastened aft and reported to the mate. I told him that nothing could be seen, but that the sounds apparently came from right ahead of us. On hearing this he ordered the man at the wheel to let the ship's head come off a couple of points. A moment later a shrill screaming tore its way through the night, followed by the hoarse braying sounds once more.

"It's close on the starboard bow!" exclaimed the mate, as he beckoned the helmsman to let her head come off a little more. Then, singing out for the watch, he ran forward, slacking the lee braces on the way. When he had the yards trimmed to his satisfaction on the new course, he returned to the poop and hung far out over the rail listening intently. Moments passed that seemed like hours, yet the silence remained unbroken. Suddenly the sounds began again, and so close that it seemed as though they must be right aboard of us. At this time I noticed a strange booming note mingled with the brays. And once or twice there came a sound that can only be described as a sort of "gug, gug." Then would come a wheezy whistling, for all the world like an asthmatic person breathing.

All this while the moon shone wanly through the steam, which seemed to me to be somewhat thinner. Once the mate gripped me by the shoulder as the noises rose and fell again. They now seemed to be coming from a point broad on our beam. Every eye on the ship was straining into the mist, but with no result. Suddenly one of the men cried out, as something long and black slid past us into the fog astern. From it there rose four indistinct and ghostly towers, which resolved themselves into spars and ropes, and sails.

"A ship! It's a ship!" we cried excitedly. I turned to Mr. Gray; he, too, had seen something, and was staring aft into the wake. So ghostlike, unreal, and fleeting had been our glimpse of the stranger, that we were not sure that we had seen an honest, material ship, but thought that we had been vouchsafed a vision of some phantom vessel like the Flying Dutchman. Our sails gave a sudden flap, the clew irons flogging the bulwarks with hollow thumps. The mate glanced aloft.

"Wind's dropping," he growled savagely. "We shall never get out of this infernal place at this gait!"

Gradually the wind fell until it was a flat calm. No sound broke the deathlike silence save the rapid patter of the reef points, as she gently rose and fell on the light swell. Hours passed, and the watch was relieved and I then went below. At seven bells we were called again, and as I went along the deck to the galley, I noticed that the fog seemed thinner, and the air cooler. When eight bells were struck I relieved Hansard at coiling down the ropes. From him I learned that the steam had begun to clear about four bells, and that the temperature of the sea had fallen ten degrees.

In spite of the thinning mist, it was not until about a half an hour later that we were able to get a glimpse of the surrounding sea. It was still mottled with dark patches, but the bubbling and popping had ceased. As much of the surface of the ocean as could be seen had a peculiarly desolate aspect. Occasionally a wisp of steam would float up from the nearer sea, and roll undulatingly across its silent surface, until lost in the vagueness that still held the hidden horizon. Here and there columns of steam rose up in pillars, which gave me the impression that the sea was hot in patches. Crossing to the starboard side and looking over, I found that conditions there were similar to those to port. The desolate aspect of the sea filled me with an idea of chilliness, although the air was quite warm and muggy. From the break of the poop the mate called to me to get his glasses.

When I had done this, he took them from me and walked to the taffrail. Here he stood for some moments polishing them with his handkerchief. After a moment he raised them to his eyes, and peered long and intently into the mist astern. I stood for some time staring at the point on which the mate had focused his glasses. Presently something shadowy grew upon my vision. Steadily watching it, I distinctly saw the outlines of a ship take form in the fog.

"See!" I cried, but even as I spoke, a lifting wraith of mist disclosed to view a great four-masted bark lying becalmed with all sails set, within a few hundred yards of our stern. As though a curtain had been raised, and then allowed to fall, the fog once more settled down, hiding the strange bark from our sight. The mate was all excitement, striding with quick, jerky steps, up and down the poop, stopping every few moments to peer through his glasses at the point where the four-master had disappeared in the fog. Gradually, as the mists dispersed again, the vessel could be seen more plainly, and it was then that we got an inkling of the cause of the dreadful noises during the night.

For some time the mate watched her silently, and as he watched the conviction grew upon me that in spite of the mist, I could detect some sort of movement on board of her. After some time had passed, the doubt became a certainty, and I could also see a sort of splashing in the water alongside of her. Suddenly the mate put his glasses on top of the wheel box and told me to bring him the speaking trumpet. Running to the companionway, I secured the trumpet and was back at his side.

The mate raised it to his lips, and taking a deep breath, sent a hail across the water that should have awakened the dead. We waited tensely for a reply. A moment later a deep, hollow mutter came from the bark; higher and louder it swelled, until we realized that we were listening to the same sounds we had heard the night before. The mate stood aghast at this answer to his hail; in a voice barely more than a hushed whisper, he bade me call the Old Man. Attracted by the mate's hail and its unearthly reply, the watch had all come aft and were clustered in the mizzen rigging in order to see better.

After calling the captain, I returned to the poop, where I found the second and third mates talking with the chief. All were engaged in trying to pierce the clouds of mist that half hid our strange consort and to arrive at some explanation of the strange phenomena of the past few hours. A moment later the captain appeared carrying his telescope. The mate gave him a brief account of the state of affairs and handed him the trumpet. Giving me the telescope to hold, the captain hailed the shadowy bark. Breathlessly we all listened, when again, in answer to the Old Man's hail, the frightful sounds rose on the still morning air. The skipper lowered the trumpet and stood with an expression of astonished horror on his face.

"Lord!" he exclaimed. "What an ungodly row!"

At this, the third, who had been gazing through his binoculars, broke the silence.

"Look," he ejaculated. "There's a breeze coming up astern." At his words the captain looked up quickly, and we all watched the ruffling water.

"That packet yonder is bringing the breeze with her," said the skipper. "She'll be alongside in half an hour!"

Some moments passed, and the bank of fog had come to within a hundred yards of our taffrail. The strange vessel could be distinctly seen just inside the fringe of the driving mist wreaths. After a short puff, the wind died completely, but as we stared with hypnotic fascination, the water astern of the stranger ruffled again with a fresh catspaw. Seemingly with the flapping of her sails, she drew slowly up to us. As the leaden seconds passed, the big four-master approached us steadily. The light air had now reached us, and with a lazy lift of our sails, we, too, began to forge slowly through that weird sea. The bark was now within fifty yards of our stern, and she was steadily drawing nearer, seeming to be able to outfoot us with ease. As she came on she luffed sharply, and came up into the wind with her weather leeches shaking.

I looked toward her poop, thinking to discern the figure of the man at the wheel, but the mist coiled around her quarter, and objects on the after end of her became indistinguishable. With a rattle of chain sheets on her iron yards, she filled away again. We meanwhile had gone ahead, but it was soon evident that she was the better sailor, for she came up to us hand over fist. The wind rapidly freshened and the mist began to drift away before it, so that each moment her spars and cordage became more plainly visible. The skipper and the mates were watching her intently when an almost simultaneous exclamation of fear broke from them.

"My God!"

And well they might show signs of fear, for crawling about the bark's deck were the most horrible creatures I had ever seen. In spite of their unearthly strangeness there was something vaguely familiar about them. Then it came to me that the face that Stevenson and I had seen during he night belonged to one of them. Their bodies had something of the shape of a seal's, but of a dead, unhealthy white. The lower part of the body ended in a sort of double-curved tail on which they appeared to be able to shuffle about. In place of arms, they had two long, snaky feelers, at the ends of which were two very humanlike hands, which were equipped with talons instead of nails. Fearsome indeed were these parodies of human beings!

Their faces, which, like their tentacles, were black, were the most grotesquely human things about them, and the upper jaw closed into the lower, after the manner of the jaws of an octopus. I have seen men among certain tribes of natives who had faces uncommonly like theirs, but yet no native I had ever seen could have given me the extraordinary feeling of horror and revulsion I experienced toward these brutal-looking creatures.

"What devilish beasts!" burst out the captain in disgust.

With this remark he turned to the mates, and as he did so, the expressions on their faces told me that they had all realized what the presence of these bestial-looking brutes meant. If, as was doubtless the case, these creatures had boarded the bark and destroyed her crew, what would prevent them from doing the same with us? We were a smaller ship and had a smaller crew, and the more I thought of it the less I liked it.

We could now see the name on the bark's bow with the naked eye.

It read Scottish Heath, while on her boats we could see the name bracketed with Glasgow, showing that she hailed from that port. It was a remarkable coincidence that she should have a slant from just the quarter in which yards were trimmed, as before we saw her she must have been drifting around with everything "aback." But now in this light air she was able to run along beside us with no one at her helm. But steering herself she was, and although at times she yawed wildly, she never got herself aback. As we gazed at her we noticed a sudden movement on board of her, and several of the creatures slid into the water.

"See! See! They've spotted us. They're coming for us!" cried the mate wildly.

It was only too true, scores of them were sliding into the sea, letting themselves down by means of their long tentacles. On they came, slipping by scores and hundreds into the water, and swimming toward us in droves. The ship was making about three knots, otherwise they would have caught us in a very few minutes. But they persevered, gaining slowly but surely, and drawing nearer and nearer. The long, tentacle-like arms rose out of the sea in hundreds, and the foremost ones were already within a score of yards of the ship before the Old Man bethought himself to shout to the mates to fetch up the half dozen cutlasses that comprised the ship's armory. Then, turning to me, he ordered me to go down to his cabin and bring up the two revolvers out of the top drawer of the chart table, also a box of cartridges that was there.

When I returned with the weapons he loaded them and handed one to the mate. Meanwhile the pursuing creatures were coming steadily nearer, and soon half a dozen of the leaders were directly under our counter. Immediately the captain leaned over the rail and emptied his pistol into them, but without any apparent effect. He must have realized how puny and ineffectual his efforts were, for he did not reload his weapon.

Some dozens of the brutes had reached us, and as they did so, their tentacles rose into the air and caught our rail. I heard the third mate scream suddenly, and turning, I saw him dragged quickly to the rail, with a tentacle wrapped completely around him. Snatching a cutlass, the second mate hacked off the tentacle where it joined the body. A gout of blood splashed into the third mate's face, and he fell to the deck. A dozen more of those arms rose and wavered in the air, but they now seemed some yards astern of us. A rapidly widening patch of clear water appeared between us and the foremost of our pursuers, and we raised a wild shout of joy. The cause was soon apparent; for a fine fair wind had sprung up, and with the increase in its force, the Scottish Heath had got herself aback, while we were rapidly leaving the monsters behind us. The third mate rose to his feet with a dazed look, and as he did so something fell to the deck. I picked it up and found that it was the severed portion of the tentacle of the third's late adversary. With a grimace of disgust I tossed it into the sea, as I needed no reminder of that awful experience.

Three weeks later we anchored in San Francisco. There the captain made a full report of the affair to the authorities, with the result that a gunboat was despatched to investigate. Six weeks later she returned to report that she had been unable to find any signs, either of the ship herself or of the fearful creatures that had attacked her. And since then nothing, as far as I know, has ever been heard of the four-masted bark Scottish Heath, last seen by us in the possession of creatures that may rightly be called demons of the sea.

Whether she still floats, occupied by her hellish crew, or whether some storm has sent her to her last resting place beneath the waves is surely a matter of conjecture. Perchance on some dark, fog-bound night, a ship in that wilderness of waters may hear cries and sounds beyond those of the wailing of the winds. Then let them look to it, for it may be that the demons of the sea are near them.

# JACK GREY, SECOND MATE

## *I*

HE stepped aboard from one of the wooden jetties projecting from the old Longside wharf, where the sailing ships used to lie above Telegraph Hill, San Francisco. She rejected almost disdainfully the great hand extended by the second mate to assist her over the gangway.

The big man flushed somewhat under his tan, but otherwise gave no sign that he was aware of the semi-unconscious slight. She, on her part, moved aft daintily to meet the captain's wife, under whose wing she was to make the passage from Frisco to Baltimore.

At first it seemed as if she were to be the only passenger in the big steel bark; but, about half an hour before sailing, a second appeared on the little jetty, accompanied by several bearers carrying his luggage. These, having dumped their burdens at the outer end of the gangway, were paid and dismissed; after which the passenger, a gross, burly-looking man, apparently between forty and forty-five years of age, made his way aboard.

It was evident that he was no stranger to sea-craft; for without hesitation, he walked aft and down the companionway. In a few minutes he returned to the deck. He glanced ashore to where his luggage remained piled up as he had left it, then went over to where the second mate was standing by the rail across the break of the poop.

"Here, you!" he said brusquely, speaking fair English, but with an unfamiliar accent. "Why don't you get my luggage aboard?"

The second mate turned and glanced down at him from his great height.

"Were you speaking to me?" he asked quietly. "Certainly I was addressing you, you —"

He stopped and retreated a pace, for there wassomething in the eyes of the big officer which quieted him.

"If you will go below I'll have your gear brought aboard," the second mate told him.

The tone was polished and courteous, but there was still something in the gray eyes. The passenger glanced uneasily from the eyes to the great, nervous hand lying, gently clenched, upon the rail. Then, without a word, he turned and walked aft.

\* \* \* \*

THE Carlyle had been two days at sea, and was running before a fine breeze of wind. On the poop the second mate was walking up and down, smoking meditatively. Occasionally he would go to the break and pass some order to the boatswain, then resume his steady tramp.

Presently, he heard a step on the companion stairs, and, the moment afterward, saw the lady passenger step out on deck. She was very white, and walked somewhat unsteadily, as if she were giddy.

She was followed by the captain's wife, carrying a rug and a couple of cushions. These the good woman proceeded to arrange on the captain's own deck-chair, after which she steadied the girl to a sitting position and wrapped the rug around her knees and feet.

Abruptly, in one of his periodic journeys, as the second mate passed to windward of the place where they were sitting, the voice of the lady passenger reached him. She was addressing the captain's wife, but was obviously indifferent whether he heard or not.

"I wish that man would take his horrible pipe somewhere else. The smell of it makes me quite sick!"

He was aware that the captain's wife was trying to signal to him behind the girl's back; but he made no sign that he saw. Instead, he continued his return journey to the break of the poop, with a certain grimness about the corners of his mouth.

Here he proceeded to walk athwartships, instead of fore and aft, so that now he came nowhere near to the girl whose insolent fastidiousness had twice irked him. He continued to smoke; for he was of too big a mind to give way to the smallness of being huffed over the lady's want of manners. He had removed from her presence the cause of her annoyance, and, being of a logical disposition, saw no reason for ceasing to obtain the reasonable enjoyment of his pipe.

As he made his way to and fro across the planks, he proceeded to turn the matter over in his own calm way. Evidently she regarded him — if she thought at all about him — as a kind of upper servant; this being so, it was absurd to suppose that there was an intentional rudeness, beyond such as servants are accustomed to receive in their position of living automata. And here, having occasion to go down on to the main deck to trim sail, he forgot the matter.

When he returned to the poop, the girl was sitting alone; the captain's wife having been called below to attend to her husband who had been ill enough to be confined to his bunk for upward of a week.

As he passed across the planks, he cast occasional glances aft. The girl was certainly winsome, and peculiarly attractive, to such a man as he, in her calm unknowing of his near presence. She was sitting back in the chair, leaning tiredly and staring full of thought out across the sea.

A while passed thus, perhaps the half of an hour, and then came the sound of heavy steps coming up from the saloon. The second mate recognized them for those of the male passenger; yet the girl did not seem to notice them. She did not withdraw her gaze from the sea, but continued to stare, seeming lost in quiet thought.

The man's head appeared out of the companionway, then the clumsy grossness of his trunk and fat under-limbs. He moved toward her, stopping within a couple of yards of her chair.

"And how is Miss Eversley?" the second mate heard him ask.

At his voice, the girl started and turned her head swiftly in his direction.

"You!" That was all she said; but the disgust and the undertone of something akin to fear were not lost upon the second officer.

"You thought —" began the man in tones of attempted banter.

"I thought I had seen the last of you — forever!" she cut in.

"But you see you were mistaken. If the sickness of the sea hadn't claimed you for the last two days, you would have discovered earlier that regret for my absence was wasted."

"Regret!"

"My pretty child —"

"Will you go away! Go away! Go away!" She put out her hands weakly with a gesture of repulsion.

"Come, come! We shall have to see much of one another during the next few weeks. Why —"

She was on her feet, swaying giddily. He took a step forward, as if with an unconscious instinct to bar her passage.

"Let me pass!" she said, with a little gasp.

But he, staring at her with hot eyes, seemed not to have heard her. She put up a hand to her throat, as if wanting air.

"Allow me to assist you below."

It was the deep voice of the second mate. His naturally somewhat grave face gave no indication that he was aware of any tensions.

"I will attend to that," said the male passenger insolently.

But the officer seemed to have no knowledge of his existence. Instead, he guided the lady to the companionway, and then down the stairs to the saloon. There he left her in the charge of the captain's wife, telling the latter that the sea air had proved too much for the young lady.

Returning on deck, he found the passenger standing by the opening of the companion. He had it in his heart to deal with the person in a fashion of his own; but the fellow had taken the measure of the big officer and, though full of repressed rage, took good care to invite no trouble.

On his part, the second mate resumed his steady tramp of the deck; but it may be noted that his pipe went out twice, for his thoughts were upon the girl he had helped below. He was pondering the matter of her repulsion for the male passenger. It was evident that they had met elsewhere, probably at the port where the Carlyle had picked them up. It was even more evident that the girl had no desire to continue the acquaintance, if it could be named as such.

Upon this, and much more to the same effect, did he meditate. And so, in due time, the first mate came up to his relief.

## II

THREE days later, the captain died suddenly, leaving his wife helpless with grief at her loss. By this time, Miss Eversley had gathered strength after her bout with seasickness, and now did her best to comfort the poor woman. Yet the desolate wife would not be comforted, but took to her bunk as soon as her husband had passed into the deep, and there stayed, refusing to be companied by any one. This being so, Miss Eversley was, perforce, left greatly to her own devices, and her own company; for that of Mr. Pathan, the other passenger, she avoided in a most determined manner.

This was by no means an easy matter to accomplish, save by staying in her berth; for did she go upon the poop, the man would, in defiance of all her entreaties or commands, pursue her with his hateful attentions. Yet help was to come; for it happened one day that, the poop being empty save for the man at the wheel, with whom, however, Pathan seemed curiously familiar, the fellow took advantage of the opportunity to try to take her hands. He succeeded in grasping her left, making the remark:

"Don't be so skittish, my pretty. What are your hands, when I am to have the whole of you?" And he laughed mockingly.

For answer, she tried to pull away from him, but without success.

"You see, it's no good fighting against me!"

She glanced round, breathlessly, for help and her gaze fell upon the helmsman, a little, hideous dago who, with an evil grin upon his face, was watching them. At that, she went all hot with shame and anger.

"Let go of my hand!"

"I shall not!"

He reached his left out for her right, but she drew it back; and then, as if with the reflex of the movement, clenched it and struck him full in the mouth.

"Beast!" she said with a little savage note in her voice.

The man staggered a moment; for the blow had been shrewdly delivered, and his surprise almostequaled the pain. Then he came back at her with a rush. The man was no better than some bestial creature at the moment. He seized her about the neck and the waist.

"D— you!" he snarled. "I'll teach —"

But he never finished. A great knuckled hand came between their faces, splaying itself across his forehead. His sweating visage was wrenched from hers. A rough, blue-sleeved arm comforted his neck mightily, tilting his chin heavenward. His grip weakened upon her, then gave abruptly, and she staggered back dizzily against the mizzen rigging.

There came a sound of something falling. It was a very long distance away. She was conscious of the second mate in the immediate foreground, his back turned to her; and beyond him, her gross-featured antagonist huddled limply upon the deck. For a moment neither moved; then the man upon the deck rose shakily, keeping his eye mateward.

The big officer never stirred, and the passenger began backing to get the skylight between him and the second mate. He reached the weather side and paused nervously. Then, and not till then, the officer turned his back upon him, and, without vouchsafing a glance in the direction of the girl, walked forward toward the break of the poop.

As she made to go below, she heard the little steersman mutter something to the defeated man; and he, now that he was in no instant danger of annihilation, raised his voice to a blusterous growl. But the big man?

### III

THE fore-hands of the big steel bark Carlyle were a new lot who had been signed on in Frisco, in place of the outward-bound crew of Scotch and Welsh sailormen, who had deserted on account of the high pay ruling in Frisco. The present crowd was composed chiefly of "Dutchmen," and in each watch, consisting of eight men and a boy, there were only two Americans, one Englishman and a German. The remainder were dagoes and mixed breeds.

The two Americans were in the first mate's watch, the Englishman and the German being with the second's crowd, and the whole lot of them, white, olive and mixed, were about as hard a "rough-house" crew, scraped up from the waterfront, as one could find, and acceptable only because of the aforementioned high wages and shortage of men.

And, to complete the number of undesirables aboard, there was Mr. Pathan, the half-breed passenger.

Finally, Mr. Dunn, the first mate, was a nervous little man, totally unfitted to handle anything more than an orderly crew of respectable Scandinavians. The result was that already his own watch had been once so out of hand he had been forced to call upon the second officer to help him maintain authority; since when, automatically, as it were, the second mate had taken, though unofficially, the reins of authority into his own hands.

Thus the situation five days after leaving port, on the homeward passage.

A week had passed.

"If you please, sir, I'd like a word with you."

It was the big boatswain who spoke. He had come halfway up the poop ladder, and his request was put in a low voice, yet with an apparently casual air.

"Certainly, Barton! Come up here if you have anything about which you wish to speak."

"It's about the men, sir. There's something up, an' I can't just put me finger on it."

"How do you mean, something up?"

"Well, sir, they're gettin' a bit at a loose end, an' they're gettin' a bit too free-like with their lip if I tells 'em to do anythin'."

"Well, you know, Barton, I cannot help you in that. If you cannot keep them in hand without aid, you'll never do it with."

"'Tisn't exactly that, sir. I can handle a crowd right enough along with any man; savin' it be yourself, sir" — with an acknowledging glance at his officer's gigantic proportions — "but there's somethin' in the wind, as is makin' 'em too ikey. It's only since the cap'n went, an' it's my belief as yon passenger's at the bottom of it!"

"Ah!"

"You noticed somethin' then, sir?" asked the boatswain quickly.

"Tell me what makes you think the passenger may be in anything that is brewing?" said the second mate, ignoring the man's question.

"Well, for one thing, sir, he's too familiar with the men. An' I've seen him go forrard to the fo'cas'le of a night when 'twas dark. Once I went up to the door on the quiet, thinkin' as I'd get to see what it was as he was up to; but the chap on the lookout spotted me an' started talkin'. I reckonedhe meant headin' me off; so I asked him to pass me down the end of me clothesline, for a bluff, an' then I made tracks."

"But didn't you get any idea of what the fellow was doing in the fo'cas'le?'"

"Well, sir, it seemed to me as he was palaverin' to 'em like a father; but as I was sayin' I hadn't time to get the bearin's of what was goin' forrard. Then there's another matter, sir, as —"

"And you might tell the man, while he's up, to take a look at the chafing gear on the fore swifter," interjected the second mate calmly.

The irrelevancy of this remark seemed to bring the boatswain up all standing, as the saying goes. He glanced up at the officer's face, and in so doing the field of his vision included something else — the very one of whom they were talking. He understood now the reason of the second's apparently causeless remark; for that keen-sensed officer had detected the almost cat-like tread approaching them along the poop-deck, and changed the conversation on the instant.

For a couple of minutes the boatswain and the second mate kept up a talk upon certain technical details of ship work, until Mr. Pathan was out of hearing.

"I reckon as he thought he'd like to know what it was we're talkin' about, sir," remarked the boatswain, eying the broad back of the stout passenger.

"What is this other matter that you want to speak to me about?"

"Well, sir, some of the hands 'as got hold of booze somehow. I keeps smellin' of 'em whenever one of 'em comes near me, and I reckon as he" — jerking his head in the direction of Mr. Pathan — "is the one as is givin' it to 'em."

The second mate swore quietly.

"What's his game, sir? That's what's foozlin' me. I thinks it's time as you looked inter ther matter!"

"If I thought —"

"Yes, sir?" encouraged the boatswain.

But whatever the second mate thought, he did not put it into words. Instead, he asked the boatswain if he were of the opinion that any of the forecastle crowd were to be depended upon.

"Not one of 'em, sir! There isn't one as wouldn't put a knife inter you if he got half a chanst!"

The second nodded, as if the man's summing-up of the crew were in accordance with his own ideas. Then he spoke.

"Well, Barton, I cannot do anything till we know more definitely what is in the wind. You must keep your eyes open and report to me anything that seems likely to help."

Behind them they heard again the pad of Mr. Pathan's deck shoes.

"You had better overhaul the sheaves in those main lower topsail brace blocks," he remarked for the benefit of the listening passenger. "That will do for the present."

"Very good, sir," said the boatswain, and went down the ladder on to the main deck.

IV

IT was in the afternoon watch, and Miss Eversley was sitting with a book in her lap, staring thoughtfully out across the sea.

Forward of her, the second mate tramped across the break of the poop. When she had appeared on deck, he had been pacing fore and aft along the poop, but had kept since then to the fore part of the deck.

Of the male passenger there was no sign. Indeed, since the big officer's "handling" of him, he had kept quite away from her, so that at last she was beginning to find her stay aboard not at all unpleasant. Occasionally the girl's glance would stray inboard to the great silent man, smoking and meditating as he paced across the planks.

It was curious (she recognized the fact) how often of late she had found her thoughts dwelling upon him. He was no longer a nonentity — something below the line of her horizon — but a man, and a man in whom she was beginning to be interested. She remembered now — what at the time she had scarcely noticed — her casual ignoring of his proffered aid as she stepped aboard. It had seemed nothing then to her, no more than if she had casually rejected the aid of a footman; but now she could not comprehend how she had done it.

From this her memory led her to that distinctly to-be-regretted remark about his smoking. She watched him, and realized the more completely as she did so that she would be vitally afraid to do such a thing again; for, all unaware to herself, the manhood of the man was mastering her. Yet, at this time, she had no realization of the fact; nothing beyond that she was interested in him, perhaps somewhat afraid and certainly a little desirous of knowing him.

On the second mate's part, he was thinking of other things than her. The preceding day he had been obliged to step down on the main deck to exert authority, and had succeeded only by laying out a couple of the crew. That the disaffection was due, in part at least, to Mr. Pathan he had very little doubt; but no proof that would justify him in putting the man in irons, as he had determined to do the very moment such was forthcoming. Also, he knew that the captain's death had unsettled them, and that there were vague ideas among them that now they were under no compulsion to obey orders. It was doubtless, along these lines that

Pathan was working with them, and the thought made the big officer grit his teeth.

"Look out, Mr. Grey!"

The words came shrill and sudden in the voice of Miss Eversley, and the second officer turned sharply from where he had stopped a moment to lean upon the rail. He saw that she was on her feet, her arm extended toward him, while her gaze flickered between him and aloft. In the same instant, there was a sort of sogging thud behind him.

His stare had followed the girl's, and for an instant he had seen the dark face of one of the crew over the belly of the mizzen topsail; then he had twisted quickly to see the reason of that noise, though already half comprehending the cause. In that portion of the rail over which he had just been leaning was stuck a heavy steel marlinspike, the sharp point thereof appearing below, for it had penetrated right through the thick teak.

For a moment he looked at it, while his face grew quietly grim. Then he turned and walked toward the mizzen rigging. From here he could look up abaft the mast. Thus he saw the man who had dropped the spike making his way rapidly from aloft.

Getting into the lower rigging, the man — who proved to be one of those the second mate had floored the previous day — called out in broken English his regret for the accident; but the officer, knowing how little of an accident there had been about the affair, said nothing. Then, as soon as the creature put foot on the deck, he caught him by the nape of the neck and walked him forward to where the spike stood up in the rail.

Below on the main deck stood several of the crew, watching what would happen, and fully prepared to make trouble if they got the half of a chance. They saw the second officer grasp the embedded spike with one great hand, then with apparent ease bend it from side to side till it broke, leaving in the rail that portion which had penetrated.

Immediately afterward, quite coolly, and calculating the force of the blow, he struck the man with it upon the side of the head, so that he went limp in his grasp; then he laid him down gently on the hencoop and bade a couple of them come up and carry him to his bunk. And this, being thoroughly cowed, as was the second mate's intention, they did without so much as a murmur.

As soon as the men were gone with their burden, he walked aft to where the girl stood.

"Thank you, Miss Eversley," he said simply. "I should have been spitted like a frog if you had not called."

She made no pretense of replying, and he looked at her more particularly. She was extraordinarily pale, and staring at him out of frightened eyes. He noticed also that she held to the edge of the skylight as if for support.

"You are not well?" he said, and made as if to support her.

But she warded him off with a gesture.

"What a brute you are!" she said in a voice that would have been cold had it been less intense.

He looked at her a moment before he replied, as if weighing the use of speech.

"You don't understand," he remarked at last, calmly. "We have a rough crowd to handle, and half measures would be worse than useless. Won't you sit down?" And he indicated the chair behind her.

"It — it was butchery!" she remarked with a sort of cold anger, and ignoring his suggestion.

"Very nearly — if you hadn't called." There had come a suggestion of humor about the corners of his mouth.

"I —"

She groped backward vaguely for the chair, and seemed unconscious that it was his hands which guided her there.

"Now, see here, Miss Eversley. You must really allow me to be the better judge in a matter of this sort. I cannot afford to sign for the long trip, if only for your sake."

"For my sake!" Her voice sounded scornful. "Inwhat way does it concern me?"

The grimness crept back into his face and chased away the scarcely perceptible humor.

"In this way," he replied in a voice as nearly as cold as her own but for a certain almost savage intensity. "I, and I alone, am keeping matters quiet aboard here; for I may as well tell you at once that the first mate does not count for that much" — and he snapped his finger and thumb — "among the crowd we've got in this packet. They're quiet at present only because they're afraid of me."

"What do you mean?" She asked the question with a brave assumption of indifference, to which her frightened eyes gave no support. "How does it matter to me whether your men are quiet or not?"

He looked at her a moment quietly and with something in the expression of his face that would have been contempt had it not been tempered by a deeper emotion.

"Listen!" he said, and she quailed before his masterfulness. "If that spike had done its work just now, you had been better dead than here.

Do you think —"

He did not finish but turned from her and walked forward along the deck, leaving her gazing at the nakedness of a hideous possibility.

## V

A WEEK passed in quietness, and, though the second mate and the boatswain between them had kept a strict watch upon the male passenger's movements, there had been nothing that could be looked upon with suspicion; for they had no knowledge of the tightly folded notes flipped to the helmsman, and by him conveyed forward, and read for the delectation of the mutinous crowd in the forecastle.

It was extraordinary that Pathan should discontinue so abruptly his nocturnal visits to the men. Possibly he had caught a stray word or two of the boatswain's confabulation with the second mate, and so taken fright. Whatever it was, the fact remained that it was impossible to come upon anything which would justify their putting him out of the way of doing mischief. Even the boatswain's complaints about the men's behavior seemed to be lacking foundation during this time, and altogether the ship appeared to be quieting down nicely.

Though there had seemed of late little need for anticipating trouble, yet the second mate had his doubts but that there was something under this apparent calm, and, having his doubts, took the precaution to carry a companionable weapon in his side pocket.

In the end, events proved that he was right; for, one afternoon on watch, the boatswain, chancing to have physical trouble with one of the men, the rest of the watch closed in upon him in a mob. At that the second mate went down to take a turn, which turn he took to such a tune that he had three of them stretched out before they were well aware that he was among them. They were beginning to give before his onslaught when suddenly he heard Pathan's voice, away aft, singing out:

"Get on to him, lads! Now's your time! Give the bully a taste of his own sort!"

At that the rest of them turned upon him with a rush, leaving the sadly mauled boatswain to himself. And now the second mate showed of what he was made. They were clinging on to him like a lot of weasels — gripping his legs to trip him, grasping at his hands and arms, and climbing on his back. One of these latter having clasped hands under his chin, was doing his utmost to throttle him.

This the second mate foiled by unclasping the fellow's dirty paws and pulling him bodily over his head, bringing him, with a continuation of the movement, crashing down upon those of his attackers immediately in front. At the same instant, the boatswain, being by now somewhat recovered, laid hold upon one of those in the rear and hauled him off. Even as he did so, there came the sound of a pistol shot.

The second mate hove himself round carrying the mass of clinging men with him. He saw Pathan coming along the decks toward them at a run. In his hand was a pistol, with the smoke still rising from it. Upon the deck lay the boatswain. He was kicking and twitching; for it was he whom the passenger had shot.

"You d—d skunk!" roared the second mate. He caught two of his attackers by the hair of their heads and beat their skulls together so they became immediately senseless.

He saw Pathan halt within a dozen feet of him and aim straight at his head. He had been dead the following instant, but that there happened a diversion.

A white face flashed into the field of his vision, and the next moment Miss Eversley had thrown ahandful of some whitish powder into the man's face. The pistol dropped with a thud, and from Pathan there was nothing save a mixture of gasps and shouts, violent sneezing, and coughs that broke off oddly into breathless blasphemy.

The second mate shouted incoherently. Then the girl was upon his assailants, throwing handfuls of the powder into their faces; whereupon they loosed him, as if their strength had gone from them, and fell to much the same antics as had Pathan. Some of the powder rose and assailed the second officer's nostrils, so that he sneezed violently. It was pepper!

He turned to the girl. At her feet lay the tin with which she had wrought his relief. She herself was standing, crying and sneezing along with the rest, and trying to wipe her eyes with a peppery handkerchief.

The second mate's glance noted the pistol dropped by Pathan, and he stepped over, and, picking it up, put it in his pocket. Between him and the group of sneezing, choking men lay the body of the boatswain. A lot of the pepper had been spilt upon his upturned face, yet he moved no whit. He was quite dead.

"What's happened, Mr. Grey?" asked a thin voice at his elbow.

"Rank mutiny!" he replied.

"Whatever shall we do?" returned the voice, the owner of which was the first mate. "Whatever shall we do?"

"Nothing," said the second mate shortly.

He turned from the mate and bellowed to the other watch who were coming aft in a body, having been aroused by the noise.

"Now then, my lads! Up forrard with you! Smartly!" And he pulled out his revolver.

They went backward with a surge as he covered them.

"Back into the fo'cas'le! Don't stir out till I tell you!"

The threatening weapon, backed by the determination of the man, overawed them and they went quickly.

"Close that door!" he roared.

It was closed immediately. Then he turned his attention to those around. Miss Eversley was standing near, her cheeks white, but her eyes and nose very red. It was plain to him that she was all of a tremble and like to fall, so that, without more ado, he took her by the shoulders and led her to a seat upon a spar lashed along by the bulwarks.

"Now, don't faint," he commanded.

"I'm not going to," she said soberly.

He left her hurriedly; for the men, having recovered from the effects of the pepper, were gathered in a clump and eying him doubtfully. To the right, Pathan had got upon his feet. It is just possible that in another moment they would have been upon him, which would have meant the loosing of the other watch, had he not acted with decision.

"Cyrone and Andy," he shouted, facing them squarely, "aft with you, and tell the steward to pass out the irons!"

At the word, Andy started aft to obey. But Cyrone, one of those who had been foremost in the trouble, made no move.

"Cyrone!" said the second mate.

The man had done well to understand the dangerous quiet in his tone; but he did not. Instead, with unbounded insolence, he turned to the fellows surrounding him.

"Who for the irons, hey? They for we! I know! I know!" he shouted excitedly, and broke off into an unintelligible jargon of words.

"Cyrone!"

"For to h— you go!" shouted the wretch in reply. It was evident that he was depending on the others to back him up.

The second mate said no word, but raised his pistol. The men about Cyrone scattered to each side. They had seen the second mate's eyes. In that last moment the fellow himself must have come suddenly into knowledge; for he started back, crying out something in an altered tone.

There was a scream from Miss Eversley, which blent with the sudden crack of the weapon; then Cyrone staggered and fell sideways on to the hatch. There was an instant of strange silence, broken by a dullish thud on the deck behind.

"Jardkenoff, go along with Andy for those irons," said the second mate in a level tone.

At his order the whole of them had started forward like frightened animals.

Jardkenoff ran past him, crying "Yi, yi, sir!" in a shaking voice.

While they were gone for the irons, the second mate bade the others lift the bodies of the boatswain and Cyrone on to the hatch. Then he looked round to discover the cause of that thud upon the deck. He saw that Miss Eversley had fallen forward off the spar on to her face, and at that he hastened to lift her. Fortunately, she had escaped injury, at which unconsciously he sighed relief. Then, taking her into his arms, he carried her to the hatch, singing out to one of the men by name to run aft to bring the steward with some brandy.

All this while, Pathan, the passenger, had stood in a dazed fashion beside the main-mast. Now, thinking he perceived a chance to steal aft to the temporary safety of his room, he began to sidle quietly away. It was no use, for the mate's voice pulled him up short before he had gone a dozen feet.

"You will stay where you are, Mr. Pathan!" was all that he said.

When the irons came, the steward accompanied them, carrying a glass full of brandy. This, under the eye of the second mate, he proceeded to administer. At the same time, the officer was superintending the ironing of Pathan. By the time that this was accomplished, Miss Eversley had begun to come to a knowledge of her surroundings, and presently sat up. Before this, however, the second mate had seen to it that Pathan was removed to the lazarette, for he would not have her upset further by sight of the murderer.

As soon as she was strong enough, he gave her his arm and led her aft to her cabin. In the saloon they came upon the captain's wife sitting limply in one of the chairs. At their entrance, she started up, and cried out something in a frightened voice. The poor woman seemed demented and quite incapable of rational speech. It was evident that the scene on deck — which apparently she had witnessed — had, in conjunction with her recent loss, temporarily unsettled her mental balance.

With difficulty they persuaded her to go to her room, after which the second mate returned to the deck, with the intention of trying to put a little heart into the nonentity whom Fate had placed above him in the scale of authority.

That evening, in the second dog-watch, the body of Cyrone was, by his orders, ignominiously dumped over the side without ceremony, and with a piece of rope and holystone attached to his feet.

## VI

THE following day it was a somewhat cowed lot of men who came aft, at the second mate's bidding, to the funeral of the boatswain. Nor did his opinion of them, expressed tersely after the body had gone down into the darkness, help to reassure them. He told them that, at the first sign of further insubordination, he would shoot them down like the dogs they were; that, in future, there should be no afternoon watch below, and that work should be continued right through the two dog-watches. On learning this, there came a slight murmur, expressive of discontent checked by fear, from the men grouped below the break.

"Silence!" roared the second officer, and whipped out a pistol from his side pocket.

Instantly the murmur ceased; for the men, as was the second's intention, realized that he would stop nowhere to enforce his commands. And there was still vividly in their minds the execution of Cyrone.

As the men went forward, the first mate ventured a weak protest against the second's measures.

"You'll have 'em murdering us, Mr. Grey, if you go on like that! Why don't you speak to 'em nicely?"

The second mate looked down upon his superior. At first his glance denoted impatient contempt; but after the first moment an expression of tolerance spread over his features as he took in the other's almost pathetic weakness of face and figure.

"I believe you read the Bible, Mr. Dunn?"

"I — I —" began the mate, flushing slightly. "Yes — perhaps I do sometimes. Why?"

"Well, you should know how little use swine have for pearls."

"You think, then, Mr. Grey —"

"I'm certain. That scum would take kindness for a sign of weakening on our part, and then —" He made an expressive gesture.

"I wish to God we were home!" said the mate fervently.

"You cheer up, mister!" replied the big officer. "If you have any trouble with your lot, don't stop to talk — shoot!"

"It's an awful thing to take a life."

"It is a necessary thing sometimes. And, besides, you have only to bang on the deck for me, and I'll be up in a brace of shakes."

And so, after a few more words of encouragement to the frightened man, the second left him in charge, and went below for a sleep.

True to his word, the second mate kept the mutinous crowd of sailormen hard at it from dawn to dusk. Even the first mate, inspired by his example and encouragement, made a brave attempt to follow in his wake. As the second mate put it, "Sweat the flesh off their bones, and they'll be too tired to use their dirty brains." Also, he was the more confident of keeping them in subjection, now that Pathan was safely ironed in the lazarette.

Thus, at last, matters seemed in a fair way to tend to a happy ending of the troubles that had beset them so far. Yet of one person this could not be said; for the mental condition of the captain's wife showed no signs of improvement. Fortunately, she was in no way violent and gave little trouble, her state being that of one suffering from melancholia in one of its quieter forms.

Then one morning it was discovered she was missing. A search was made through the ship, but without success. She was never found. Evidently the poor creature had crept on deck some time during the night and gone overboard.

From this, onward, nothing disturbed the monotony of the voyage for many days. The second mate kept the crew well in hand, in no way abating rigorous treatment of them, so that did he but raise a hand they jumped to do his bidding.

And now of Miss Eversley. Day by day the girl had found her thought centering upon the second mate. The horizon of her mind seemed bounded by him. She caught herself watching his least gesture as he paced the poop in his meditative fashion, or gave some order to the crew. Did the first mate relieve him, so that he could go below for a sleep, the deck seemed strangely empty, the wind chilly, the sea dull and uninteresting. Yet when he relieved the first mate, how different! Then the wind was warm, the sea full of an everlasting beauty, the deck, nay, the very planks of the deck, companionable.

And so she grew into the knowledge that she loved him, even to the extent of looking forward to her future life as a hideous blank, if he were not to share it; while he — silly man! He would break off his walks to sit and chat with her; but of that which she most desired to hear, not a word. Yet, by his eyes, she guessed that he cared; but for some reason — possibly because she was so much alone — he said nothing.

And so, at last, she might have come to aid him in spanning the gulf that remained yet between them; but that fate, in its own terrible way, took a hand.

# VII

"MR. GREY! Mr. Grey! Jack! Jack!"

The second mate woke with a start and leapt up in his bunk.

Miss Eversley was standing in the doorway of his berth.

"Quick! They've killed the first mate! And they're coming down — now! Pathan has been let out, and he's with them!"

Even before she had made an end of speaking, the second mate had reached the floor with a bound. He snatched the revolver from under his pillow, and ran into the saloon.

From the doorway, giving into the companion stairs came the sounds of whispering, and the padding of many bare feet descending. He made a quick step to meet them; but the girl caught his arm.

"Don't, Jack! Don't!" Then, as he still hesitated: "For my sake — remember! Oh! Is there no place?"

She stopped, for the second mate had caught her by the arm and was running her toward the fore part of the saloon. His wits, slightly bewildered by sleep, had flashed instantly to their normal clearness under the stress of her terror. He realized that, for her sake alone, he had no right to throw away his chances of life.

Just as the foremost of the mutineers stepped silently into the dimly lighted saloon, the big officer pushed open the door of the foremost berth on the port side and thrust Miss Eversley in. At the same moment, the man at the other end discovered them and gave a yell to announce the fact.

The following instant he lay dead, and the man behind him shared the same end. This caused a temporary hesitation on the part of the attackers, and in that slight interval the second officer slipped into the berth after the girl, slammed the door, and locked it.

"Stand to one side," he whispered to her.

As she did so, he hurled himself at the forward bulkhead of the berth. One of the boards started, and he attacked it again, the noise he was making drowning that of the mutineers in the saloon.

Crash! The momentum of his effort had made a great breach in the woodwork and taken him clean through into the absolute darkness of the sail-locker beyond.

In a moment he was back. He caught the girl by the wrist and helped her through. Even as he did sothere came a loud report in the saloon, and a bullet stripped off a long splinter on the inner side of the door as it came through.

Immediately, the second officer raised his weapon, and fired —

once — twice. At the second shot there came a sharp outcry from one of those beyond the door, and then three shots in quick reply. They hurt no one, for the big officer had bounded into the sail-locker. He had dropped his emptied weapon into his side pocket and was helping Miss Eversley over the great masses of stowed sails.

In the half of a minute he whispered to her to stand. An instant he fumbled, and she heard the rattle of a key. Then a square of pale light came in the darkness ahead of her, and she saw that he had opened a trap in the steel bulkhead that ran across the poop.

The following instant she was in darkness; for the huge bulk of her companion completely filled the aperture as he forced himself through. The light came again, and then she saw his head silhouetted against it in the opening.

"Give me your hand," he whispered, and the moment afterward she was standing beside him on the deck, under the break of the poop.

For an instant they stood there, scanning the decks, but every soul, saving the helmsman, had joined in the attack. Through the opening behind them came the sound of blows struck upon the door of the berth which they had just quitted. No time was to be lost; for the moment that the brutes discovered that rent in the woodwork of the berth, they would be after them.

A sudden idea came to the second officer. He shut down the door of the vertical trap and locked it. The men would search the sail-locker for them, now that it was shut and fastened; while, if he had left it open, they would have been on their track immediately.

"Forrard to the half-deck," he muttered, and they ran out into the moonlight.

Now the half-deck was a little, strongly built steel deck-house, situated about amidships. It had one steel door on the after end, and once they were in, and this shut, they would be comparatively safe, at least for the time being.

Abruptly, as they ran, there came a muffled outcry, and they knew that the door to the berth had been broken down. They reached the half-deck, and, while Miss Eversley sprang over the washboard, the officer ran to slip the hood which held the door back. Even as he reached up his hand there came a shout from the poop. They were discovered. There came a thudding of rapid feet, and he saw the whole remaining crew of the boat tumbling hurriedly down the ladder on to the main deck. At that critical instant he found that the hook was jammed. He riddled at it a moment; but still it refused to come out of its eye.

The running men were halfway to him, howling like wild beasts, and brandishing knives and belaying-pins. In desperation he caught the edge of the door, put one foot against the side of the house, and tugged. An instant of abominable suspense; then the hook gave, parting with a sharp crack. Through the very supremeness of his effort, he staggered back a couple of paces, then, before he could regain the door to shut it, a couple of the men who had outstripped the others, leaped past him and into the half-deck, with a cry of triumph.

He heard Miss Eversley scream; then a third man was upon him. The second mate tried to slam the door in his face, but the fellow jammed himself in between the door and the side of the doorway. At that the big officer caught him by the chin and the back of the head, and plucked him into the half-deck by sheer strength. Then he brought the door to, and slipped the bolt, just as the rest of the men outside hurled themselves against it.

From the girl there came a cry of warning, and, in the same instant, the loud clang of some heavy missile striking the door by his right ear. He whirled round just in time to receive the united charge of the three he had imprisoned with himself in the deck-house.

Fortunately there was a sufficiency of light in the berth; for the lamp had been left burning by the former occupants when they left to join in the attack on the afterguard.

Two of the men had their knives. The third stooped and made a grab for the iron belaying-pin which he had just thrown at the officer. Him the second mate made harmless by a kick in the face; then the other two were upon him.

He snatched at the knife-hand of the man to the right, and got him by the wrist; tried to do the same to the other and missed. The fellow dodged, rushed in and slashed the second mate's shirt open from the armpit to the waist, inflicting a long gash, but the next instant was hurled across the berth by aterrific left-hand blow.

The second mate turned upon the man whose wrist he had captured. His fingers were hurting intolerably, for the fellow was tearing at them with the nails of his loose hand so that they were bleeding in several places. He caught the wretch by the head, jammed the left arm under his chin, and leaned forward with a vast effort. There was a horrid crack, and the man shuddered and collapsed.

There came a little broken gasp of horror from the girl who was crouched up against the corner on the starboard side. The second mate turned upon her.

"Turn your face to the bulkhead, and stop your ears," he command-ed.

She shivered and obeyed, trembling and striving to stifle back a tumult of sobbing which had taken her.

The officer stooped and removed the knife from the hand of the dead man. Upon the door behind him there sounded a perfect thunder of blows. Abruptly, as he stood up the glass of the port on the starboard side was shattered, and a hand and arm came into the light.

The second mate dodged below the line of the bunkboard. There was a loud report, and a bullet struck somewhere against the ironwork. He ran close up to the bunk, still keeping out of sight, then rose upright with a sudden movement and grasped the pistol and the hand that held it, leaned forward over the bunk, and struck with his knife a little below the arm. There came a howl of pain from outside and the body fell away from the port, leaving the loaded pistol in the second mate's grasp.

Not a moment did he waste, but slammed to the iron cover over the port and commenced to screw up the fastening. It was stiff, so that he had to take both hands to it, and because of this he placed the revolver down upon the bedding of the bunk.

This came near to causing his death, for, suddenly, as he wrestled with the screw, a hand flashed over his shoulder and grabbed the weapon. Instinctively the second mate dodged and swung up a defending arm. He struck something. There was a sharp explosion close to his head, and then the clatter of the falling weapon.

By this he had got himself about and saw that the two whom he had temporarily disabled were upon him. Before he could defend himself, one of them struck him with the iron belaying-pin across his head. It sent him staggering across the floor.

As he fell, a scream from Miss Eversley pierced to his dull senses, and he got upon his knees, gasping and rocking, yet still full of the implacable determination to fight. For all his grit he would have been dead but for the girl. He had grasped the legs of one of his assailants; but was too dazed and weakened to put forth his usual strength.

The second man raised the heavy pin for another smite, but it never fell. To the second mate, wrestling pointlessly, there sounded a dull thud and a cry. Something fell upon him all of a heap, as it were, and he was brought to the deck upon his side; yet he had not relaxed his somewhat nervous grip upon the man's legs, so that the fellow came down with him.

For perhaps the half of a minute he held on stupidly while the man struggled violently to get away. Then, almost abruptly, nerve and reasoning-power came back to him, and in the same instant a violent pain smote him between the left shoulder and the neck. He got upon his knees, hurling the dead body of the other man from off his shoulders with the movement.

He was now above his opponent, and at once attempted to capture the fellow's knife. In this he was not at first successful, with the result that he sustained a second stab, this time slitting open the front of his shirt, and cutting his breast. At that, growing inconceivably furious, he regarded not the knife, but smote the man with his bare fist between the eyes and again below the ear, and so shrewd and mighty were the blows that the fellow died immediately.

Perceiving that the man was indeed dead, the second mate got himself upon his feet. He was breathing deeply, and his head seemed full of a dull ache.

He took his gaze from the bodies at his feet, and glanced around. Not two yards distant stood Miss Eversley. She had a revolver in her right hand. At that, the second mate understood how he had escaped with his life. Yet he had no thought of thanking her; for the horror in her face warned him not to do anything that might increase her realization of what she had done. Instead, he made two steps to her, and took her in his arms.

With the feel of his arms about her, she dropped the pistol and broke into violent weeping. And he, having some smattering of wisdom, held his peace for a space.

Presently the extreme agitation of the girl passed off, and she sobbed only at intervals. Later still she spoke.

"I shall never be happy again."

And still the second mate preserved the sweet wisdom of silence.

"Never, never, never!" he heard her whispering to herself.

And so, in a while, she calmed down to quiet breathing. For a space they stood thus, and on the decks all about the little house was silence, save for the occasional pad, pad, of a bare foot, as those without moved hither and thither.

## VIII

THE day had come and passed, and it was again night.

Within the house things could be seen but dimly, for the lamp was turned no more than a quarter up, and of oil they had no supply beyond the quantity within the lamp itself. Fortunately, there was no immediate need to worry about water; for the water breaker, lashed to the port end of the table, was a quarter full, owing to the boatswain's and carpenter's dislike for soap and water.

As for food, an examination of the bread barge in one of the empty lower bunks showed him that there was enough biscuit to keep the two of them crudely fed for some days, provided they were careful. In the food cupboard there was also half a bottle of ship's vinegar, about half a pound of ship salt pork, some sugar in a soup-and-bully tin, and about three pounds of black molasses in a big seven-pound pickle jar; all of these being the usual savings of rations that might be found in the food locker of any other lime-juicer, windjammer in all the seven seas.

He had, aided by the girl, bound up his wounds, which were not sufficiently serious to trouble him with anything more than a constant smarting; and though he had bled a good deal, he was so full of life and vitality that he was scarcely aware of the loss, except that he was abnormally thirsty; which fortunately the water in the breaker enabled him to quench freely. Yet, all the same he held this need somewhat in check, for they must never run short of the precious fluid.

During the day a certain amount of light had driven in between the crevices about the door. Beyond this there had been none, for the ports were all protected by their iron covers. Fortunately, as the second mate had discovered, all of them had been fastened on the preceding night, previous to their making a refuge of the house, all, that is, save the one through which they had been attacked. To this fortunate happening it is probable they owed their lives.

In the corner of the house to the right of the door there was a grim mound. The second mate had spread a couple of blankets over it to hide its full horror from the eyes of the girl; yet, by this very act, he had made it almost more unbearable than if he had left them in all the stark awesomeness of uncovered death.

Out upon the decks was quietness. Indeed, all through the day there had been but one attempt to molest them, and this the second mate had foiled by quietly opening one of the after ports and firing into the thick of the attacking party. In this way he was persuaded that he could have held the house for as long as it pleased him to do so but for the insurmountable obstacle that confronted him in the shape of lack of ammunition. Yet, even as it was, it was plain to him that the repulse he had given them was likely to keep them at a respectable distance — at least for some while. For, out of a crew of sixteen deck-hands, six had already been killed and several wounded.

In the brief time he had been at the port he had gathered something of the methods they had been about to apply to the felling of the door. They had rigged up a spar on a tackle, so as to form a rough sort of battering ram; yet, in the brief attempt that he had permitted them, the machine had proved unsuccessful, for the suspending rope had been too long, and the rolling of the ship had caused the spar to swing across the after end of the house, in the fashion of a clock pendulum, so that at one moment the business end of the ram was opposed to the door, and another to some portion of the end of the house.

In spite of the failure of the attackers, the big officer was well aware that with a more perfect appliance, and no ammunition with which to beat them off, they would not be long in forcing the door. And then...

The second night of the imprisonment had come. The second mate had gone to the door and was listening; but beyond the pad of a bare foot, or hum of hoarse voices, there was nothing to tell of the watchers about the decks.

For her part, the girl was busying herself clearing away the few eatables from which they had been making a meal. This done, she hesitated a moment, then went over to the second mate.

"Let me stay up tonight and watch, Jack. You have not had any sleep, and I have slept most of the day. I could wake you up the moment anything happened."

The big man put a hand on each side of her shoulders and looked down upon her with a grave half-smile.

"Do, Jack! You can trust me," she urged.

"Trust you, little girl," he replied. "Yes, child, with a thousand lives if I had them."

"Then you will let me stay up and watch?" He shook his head slowly.

"There will be no need tonight, at any rate. They cannot get at us without noise. We may both sleep."

This he said to quiet her entreaties; for he had no intention to allow her to sit alone in the darkness with her thoughts, and that blanket- covered mound, while he slept. More, he wished her to sleep; for he had a project which he hoped to carry out during the hours of darkness.

For a moment she stood looking up at him in the half-light. Then she slipped her hands on to his shoulders.

"Then I will say good night, Jack, for we must save the oil in the lamp."

The second mate stooped and kissed her. "Good night, Mary," he said gravely.

"Good night," she whispered, kissing him in return.

Then she left him and went behind the blanket which he had rigged up before the bunks on the starboard side.

A space of about two hours passed, during which the second mate lay awake listening. Presently, realizing that the girl was asleep, he got up and quietly opened the door of the house. He listened a minute and found no one about, then swiftly he carried out each of the dead bodies on to the deck and left them there. He returned to the house and locked the door.

All at once, from outside the door, there rose an outcry. At that, he knew that the dead had been discovered. The outcries sank to a subdued murmur; for there had come fear among the men. Yet from thence onward, the door was never left unguarded day or night.

## IX

THE morning of the fourth day of their imprisonment dawned, and the second mate was awakened by a noise of hammering close against the port on the left side of the door. He jumped from his bunk quietly, and crept softly to the one on his right. He had the revolver in his hand.

Very cautiously he unscrewed the fastening of the iron cover, and glanced out, but could see no one. For a little he listened, and between the blows he caught a murmur of talk some little distance away. Abruptly he recognized Pathan's voice. At that, quickly but silently, he unscrewed the fastening of the glass and opened it. He thrust his head out and looked to the left.

Close to him, and right in front of the door, stood one of the men. He held the muzzle of a clumsy ship's musket, the butt resting on the deck. The second mate remembered having observed this same antique weapon hanging in the steward's pantry. It was evident that they were but poorly supplied with firearms.

Beyond the guard, he made out a couple more of the men fixing a heavy piece of timber across the other port. Evidently they had hit upon this plan of preventing his interfering with their operations. With the two after ports blocked they could do much as they pleased.

Suddenly a sharp exclamation on his right startled the second officer. He glanced round. There was Pathan fumbling with his revolver.

Instantly the second mate snatched his head into the shelter of the house. Almost at the same moment there sounded a thunderous bang, close to the left. He heard Pathan give a scream of pain, breaking off into a blatter of cursing.

At the risk of his life he shoved his head out. Pathan was nursing his right hand, while big tears of pain were running down his cheeks to that strange accompaniment of blasphemy. On the deck, close to his feet, lay the shattered butt of his revolver. The second mate twisted to the left for a brief glance. He saw that the guard was sitting upon the deck, rubbing his right shoulder. He looked woefully scared, while nearby lay the cumbrous weapon with which he had been armed.

What had happened was now clear to the big officer. The man had fired at the protruding head — but a fraction too late — with the result that the bolt, with which the gun had been loaded, had strickenthe passenger's revolver, destroying it and wounding his hand.

Even as the solution came to the officer, the guard had reached for his gun and scrambled to his feet. In another moment he would have clubbed the second mate, but that a bullet sent him twitching to the deck.

The second mate turned his pistol upon Pathan. Could he but rid the ship of that fiend, all might yet be well.

Yet, as he pressed the trigger for the second time, his elbow was jogged from within the house. He swore between his teeth and tried another shot, only to be warned by the unsatisfying click of the hammer that his ammunition had come to an end.

He drew away from the port with an angry gesture, and well it was for him that he did so, for one of the two at work upon the port, seeing that the weapon was empty of cartridges, had run at him with a hammer. The blow missed, and the following instant the second mate had slammed the covers and fastened up the port.

He turned and found the girl standing by him.

"Do you know," he said a trifle sternly, "you made me miss Pathan when you touched me. If I had shot that wretch the men would have been glad enough to come to terms."

He was hot with his failure, or he had not spoken so to her. And she, having but touched him because of the fear which had seized her at his rashness in so exposing himself, burst into crying; for she had been sorely overstrained with the rough happenings of late.

At this his anger left him and he made to comfort her, so, for that morning they sat together, she taking little heed of the various sounds about the house which told him that the fiends outside were preparing to batter down the door. They had covered up the second port immediately after his closing of the cover, so that he had no means of knowing how matters were progressing beyond such as his ears, trained in ship-craft, could tell him.

Very slowly the day passed to its close. He knew that the final struggle was at hand; but he did not by any means consider their chances of life beyond hope; for he knew that the crew had been greatly reduced, so that, could he but avoid the fire of the big musket, he might slay

Pathan and put the rest to flight. Yet he had no knowledge but that the house might be their prison for a day or two longer; though, beyond that time they could not hope to stay, for of food they had but little, and less water.

The day had been a fine one, as they could tell by the light which came through the crevices around the somewhat loosely fitting door, and when at last the evening came, the girl went to the door to try to get a look at the sunset.

"Come and look, Jack," she said suddenly, after a period of silence.

He turned from the water breaker at which he was busy emptying the last few drops.

"What is it, Mary?"

His voice was perhaps a trifle uneasy, for he had made the discovery that there was left only half a pannikin of water. During the last two days of their imprisonment he had been limiting his allowance; for he would not see her stinted, and now, through some mischance, the spigot, which someone had fixed near the bottom of the little cask, had been loosened, and the small quantity of the imperative liquid which had been theirs was all squandered save for the drainings which he had emptied into the enameled mug.

He came across to where she stood. For the moment he was minded not to tell her, then, remembering because of the fiends outside, that a clear knowledge of their position was her due, he told her not only of this matter but of the likelihood of the crisis being near at hand.

When he had made an end, she reached up one hand to his shoulder, then held out the other for the mug. She drew him down to the crevice through which she had been peering.

"See," she said, "did you ever see such a sunset?" Her voice dropped. "And it may be our last, Jack." She patted his shoulder as she spoke. "You know, boy, I may be only a silly girl, but I know nothing but a miracle can save us."

It was the first time she had spoken out so plainly, and he, having nothing to answer, stared out blindly into the dying glory outside.

In a little, perhaps the half of a minute, she drew him back somewhat and held the little mug up before them.

"We will drink it together, darling," she whispered, and bent her head over and kissed the brim, then handed it to him; but he was not deceived.

"Fair play, little woman. You have drunk nothing."

He passed it back to her, and she, knowing him, sipped a little, then held it up to him and made him drink from her own hands. He was hideously thirsty, but controlled himself to one gulp only; then took the mug from her and set it down upon the table. For the end was not yet, and she might have need of it ere then.

It was almost dark in the berth, for the oil of the lamp was done this long while, the only light they had coming in through the crannies about the door.

For a while the two of them stood together. He was deep in pondering as to when the attack would come. Probably as soon as it was dark; for, of course, they could not be absolutely sure that he had no further supply of cartridges.

She for her part was leaning forward, peering through the narrow opening at the red splendor of the sun's shroud. Once or twice she ran her fingers up and down this crack, as if she would fain enlarge it. Possibly the tips showed outside, for her hands were very slender; yet, however it may have been, it is certain that one of the devils upon the deck was attracted and crept up on tiptoe. Inside, the girl, staring out, saw something come abruptly between her and the sun. The second mate saw it at the same moment, else she had been dead on the instant.

He pushed her from him, out of a line with the crack, and in so doing brought himself almost directly opposite. There came a sudden spurt of flame into the semi-darkness of the house, and a tremendous report close up against the door. The girl gave a little scream which almost drowned her lover's moan of pain, but not quite.

"You are not hurt, dearest?" she cried out loud.

For a moment he did not answer, and in that quick silence she heard a man outside laugh brutally.

The second mate had his hand up to his eyes and was very silent. In the dimness of the place she saw that he was swaying upon his feet.

"Jack," she said in an intense whisper of fear. "Are you hurt?"

She caught his wrist with a gentle hold. Still he did not reply. Beyond the door she heard the murmur of voices, and odd words and fragments of sentences drifted to her uncomprehending brain.

"— for?"

"Fiddlin' at ther door!"

"— bust! The gun's busted!"

"Thank God!" It was the second mate who had spoken, and the girl loosed her hands from his wrists in her astonishment. Then, with a sudden applying of his words to satisfy the desire of her soul —

"You are not hurt, then, dear?"

"A — a little. My eyes —"

"What? Let me see!" But he swung round from her.

"Can you get me some — something for a bandage?" There was a desperate levelness in his tone.

He took two or three uncertain steps across the floor, as if bewildered. She followed him. He took his hands from his face and moved his head from side to side, as if peering about the house. Abruptly, he turned and blundered into her clumsily. She would have fallen, but that he caught and steadied her.

"Jack! Oh, Jack!" she cried, for even in the dimness of the place she had caught a glimpse of where his eyes ought to have been.

"It's all right, little woman," he replied in a voice that was nearly steady. "I — can't see very well while the pain's bad." He had covered his face again with his hands.

She answered nothing. She was tearing one of her undergarments into strips, and trying to quiet her sobs.


## X

THE night had come. The second mate, the upper portion of his face swathed in wrappings, was seated on the sea-chest below his bunk. The girl was sitting by him, and their right hands were clasped.

The crack along the edge of the door had been stuffed up with a strip of blanket. Upon the edge of the table was stuck a tiny fragment of candle, and by the light of this she was reading slowly the betrothing passage from the Solemnization of Matrimony — that in which the man plights his troth. The second mate was repeating the words after her.

Presently they had made an end, and the girl slipped her hand gently from his; then, taking hold of his in turn, she read in a firm voice that passage in which the woman gives her troth. At the end, she released the second mate's hand and drew a ring from off one of her fingers. This she put gently into his hand. Then having given him her left, he slid the ring on her third finger, repeating themeanwhile, after her, the passage which she whispered to him.

And after that they sat a while, too full of thought for speech.

Presently the candle went out abruptly, and the two were alone in the darkness.

From the deck beyond the door came an occasional mutter of speech, an occasional padding of feet and an occasional creaking of gear, and the two within sat and waited.

Toward midnight the moon rose and limned the outline of the door in pale light. Presently the girl spoke.

"The moon has risen, Jack."

She rose from his side and moved to the door. Perhaps she might be able to see what the crew were busied at. Abruptly, as she stooped forward to peer, something struck the door a tremendous blow, filling the interior of the house with a deafening, hollow boom. She cried out in fear, and even as she cried came the second blow and the crack of a breaking rivet.

She realized that the attack had begun, and groped a moment for the matches. She struck one and examined the door. To the casual glance it was unharmed; but by the light of the third match she made out that a rivet in the bottom hinge was snapped. By this, a dozen blows had been dealt, and yet, from the second mate, seated upon the sea-chest, no sound.

All at once he spoke.

"Come here, Mary."

She came to him quickly, wondering, half-consciously, at the strange harshness of his tone. By the light of the match which she carried, she saw that he had in his hand the revolver.

"It's no good, Jack," she said despairingly, thinking he had a mind that she should use it in their defense. "There are no cartridges!"

"I kept — one," he said with a jerk, and still in that unnatural voice.

He reached out his left hand to her. And at that she comprehended, and comprehending shrank back with a little wail.

"O-o-h! O-o-h! Jack!" she sobbed, with a sudden plumbing of the abyss of mortal terror.

There came a louder crash on the door, and then the second mate's voice.

"Mary!"

She went up to him, quivering.

"Not yet, Jack! Not yet!"

He put his left arm round her.

"Mary!" he said, and the fierce agony which possessed him spoke out in his voice. "Tell me when the door begins to go!"

And she knew that the time of the door's standing was the span of her life.

At each ringing thud of the ram she could feel the place quiver. By now it had become a steady, almost rhythmic boom, boom, boom, which, as a rivet gave, blent into a crash. The inside of the steel house was like the inside of a great drum.

And so a minute passed, and another, and still the door stood, while that dread booming beat out the knell of the two within — he grim for very fear of himself, and she shaking because of the thing that was to happen, and still with some room in her soul for his sufferings, yet unable to say anything; for in those last moments he had become her executioner as well as her lover, and there were things she could not say to the two.

Boom! Boom! Boom! Crash!

"Mary?" His voice sounded like the cry of a lost soul, and the love in the woman answered to it. Yet the physical terror of death was upon her.

"The — the door — is — is — stop! It's only the bottom hinge has broken. It isn't down yet!" *Crash! Crash! Crash!*

The girl, all of a shiver, turned suddenly and put her arms round his neck.

"Kiss me, Jack!"

*Crash! Crash!*

He repelled her for a moment, then, drawing her to him, kissed her good-by.

*Crash! C-r-a-s-h!*

"Don't! Don't! Not yet! It isn't down yet! Give me — give me as long as you — you can!"

For the arm about her shoulders had tightened with a sudden grip. Then abruptly —

"Have you — have you a — a — a knife, Jack?"

He took his arm from about her and brought something from behind, which he held out for her to take.

She saw it faintly by the glimmer of moonlight that came through the shaken door.

"No, no, no!" she cried, and shuddered. "You — you take it! Give me the pistol. I — I can see."

He gave up the revolver to her and shifted the knife to his right hand. Even as he did so, the door crashed in. He felt the girl thrill in the grip of his arm; then her right hand went up, and, an instant later came the click of the hammer, but no report — the cartridge had missed fire. She had aimed at a dark figure beyond the doorway, which she had recognized as Pathan. Yet the cruelty of fate denied her even the consolation of knowing that she died leaving her lover not at the mercy of that creature.

She cried out her dismay, and then again in terror, for the grip of the second mate's arm warned her that the end had indeed come. There came the rush of feet along the deck, and the blaze of a flare. Then Pathan's voice:

"Don't hurt the girl!"

She caught so much of it. Then the touch of her lover's fingers upon her breast made her quiver. She felt his right arm go back for the blow.

"Oh, my God, help me! Help me! Help me!" he heard her whispering desperately, and it shook him badly in that supreme moment. But, for the love he bore her, he meant that there should be no faltering in his stroke. Abruptly, the girl felt him start violently, and he began to quiver from head to feet. He cried out something in a strange voice.

"Oh, my God!" he said in a sort of whispering, husky shout. "I can see! I can see! Oh, my God, I can see! We're going to win! Mary, Mary! we're going to win! I can see! I can see! I can see! I tell you, I can see!"

He loosed her and put both his hands up to his bandages, which had slid down on to his nose, and tore them away in a mad kind of fashion, while the girl stood limp and sick against him, still half-fainting.

"I can see! I can see!" he began to reiterate again.

He seemed to have gone momentarily insane with the enormous revulsion from utter despair to hope. Suddenly he caught the girl madly into his arms, staring down at her through the darkness. He hugged her savagely to him, whispering hoarsely his refrain of:

"I can see! I can see! I tell you I can see!"

He held her a single instant or two like this; then he literally tossed her into one of the upper bunks.

"Don't move!" he whispered, his voice full of the most intense purpose. "I'm going to get square with that brute now. There's a chance for both of us. Here, take the knife in case I don't manage. Just lie still, whatever happens. You must be out of the way. I could tackle a hundred of them now."

He was silent, listening. By the sound of the men's voices, the second mate knew that they had halted some little distance from the doorway. There they hung for a few moments, no man anxious to be the first to face the big officer. For they had no knowledge of his blindness.

Then he caught Pathan's voice urging them on. "Go on, lads! Go on! There won't be much fight left in him!"

At that, a feeling of dismay filled him. It was evident that Pathan was not going to head the attack, and he might die without ever getting his hands on to him.

From the irresolute men came a shuffle of feet. Then a man's voice rose

"Trow de flare into ze hoose."

To the second mate the remark suggested a course of action. He threw himself upon a sea-chest, so that his face could be seen from the doorway. He kept perfectly still. If the man threw the flare into the house they would see his damaged face and think him dead. It might be that the coward Pathan would venture to come into the place — then!

Thud! Something struck the floor near him.

He kept his eyes shut. He could see no light; but the smell of burning paraffin was plain in his nostrils. He listened intently and seemed to catch the sound of stealthy footsteps. Abruptly, a voice just without the doorway shouted:

"They're both dead! Both of 'em!"

"What?"

It was Pathan's voice. He heard the noise of booted feet approaching at a run. They hesitated one instant on the threshold, then came within, and a surge of barefoot pads followed. The booted feet came to a stand not two yards away.

For an instant there was silence, a bewildered, awestruck silence. Pathan's voice broke it.

"My God!" he said. "My God!"

Immediately afterward he screamed, as the huge, bloodstained form of the big officer hurled itself upon him. There were cries from the men, and a pell-mell rush to escape. Someone fell upon the flare and extinguished it.

There was a shivering silence. It was filled abruptly by the beginning of a sobbing entreaty from Pathan. This shrilled suddenly into a horrid screaming. The men were no longer trying for the doorway, for the second mate had got between it and them. They could see him indistinctly against the moonlight beyond. He was flogging the steel side of the house with something. Beyond the hideous thudding of the blows, the house was silent.

One of the crouched men, tortured to madness, threw a belaying-pin. The next instant the second mate hurled himself among them. He had the battered steel door for a weapon, and the edge of it was as a plowshare amidst soil.

Amid the cries of the men, the side of the house rang out a dull thunder beneath the weight of some blind, misdirected blow.

Most of the men escaped upon their hands and knees, creeping out behind the man who smote and smote. They got to the forecastle upon all fours, too terrified and bewildered even to get to their feet. There, in the darkness, behind closed and barred doors, they sat and sweated, in company of those who had hesitated to enter the house.

Presently the ship was quiet.

The berserker rage eased out of the second mate and he perceived that the house was empty, and the mutiny truly ended. He cast the heavy steel door clanging through the open doorway, out on to the main deck, a dripping testimony of a man's prowess against enormous odds.

He stood a moment, breathing heavily. Then, remembering, he wheeled round in the darkness to where, in the gloom of the upper bunk, the girl lay shivering, with her hands pressed tightly over her ears.

He caught her up in his great arms, with the one word, "Come!" and stepped through the open doorway into the moonlight, the fallen door ringing under his tread. Then, master of his ship, he carried her aft to the cabin.

# THE STONE SHIP

RUM THINGS! — Of course there are rum things happen at sea — As rum as ever there were. I remember when I was in the *Alfred Jessop*, a small barque, whose owner was her skipper, we came across a most extraordinary thing.

We were twenty days out from London, and well down into the tropics. It was before I took my ticket, and I was in the fo'cas'le. The day had passed without a breath of wind, and the night found us with all the lower sails up in the buntlines.

Now, I want you to take good note of what I am going to say: —

When it was dark in the second dog watch, there was not a sail in sight; not even the far off smoke of a steamer, and no land nearer than Africa, about a thousand miles to the eastward of us.

It was our watch on deck from eight to twelve, midnight, and my look-out from eight to ten. For the first hour, I walked to and fro across the break of the fo'cas'le head, smoking my pipe and just listening to the quiet.... Ever hear the kind of silence you can get away out at sea? You need to be in one of the old-time windjammers, with all the lights dowsed, and the sea as calm and quiet as some queer plain of death. And then you want a pipe and the lonesomeness of the fo'cas'le head, with the caps'n to lean against while you listen and think. And all about you, stretching out into the miles, only and always the enormous silence of the sea, spreading out a thousand miles every way into the everlasting, brooding night. And not a light anywhere, out on all the waste of waters; nor ever a sound, as I have told, except the faint moaning of the masts and gear, as they chafe and whine a little to the occasional invisible roll of the ship.

And suddenly, across all this silence, I heard Jensen's voice from the head of the starboard steps, say: —

"Did you hear *that*, Duprey?"

"What?" I asked, cocking my head up. But as I questioned, I heard what he heard — the constant sound of running water, for all the world like the noise of a brook running down a hill-side. And the queer sound was surely not a hundred fathoms off our port bow!

"By gum!" said Jensen's voice, out of the darkness. "That's damned sort of funny!"

"Shut up!" I whispered, and went across, in my bare feet, to the port rail, where I leaned out into the darkness, and stared towards the curious sound.

The noise of a brook running down a hill-side continued, where there was no brook for a thousand sea-miles in any direction.

"What is it?" said Jensen's voice again, scarcely above a whisper now. From below him on the main-deck, there came several voices questioning: — "Hark!" "Stow the talk!" ". . . there!" "Listen!" "Lord love us, what is it?" . . . And then Jensen muttering to them to be quiet.

There followed a full minute, during which we all heard the brook, where no brook could ever run; and then, out of the night there came a sudden hoarse incredible sound: — oooaze, oooaze, arrrr, arrrr, oooaze — a stupendous sort of croak, deep and somehow abominable, out of the blackness. In the same instant, I found myself sniffing the air. There was a queer rank smell, stealing through the night.

"Forrard there on the look-out!" I heard the mate singing out, away aft. "Forrard there! What the blazes are you doing!"

I heard him come clattering down the port ladder from the poop, and then the sound of his feet at a run along the maindeck. Simultaneously, there was a thudding of bare feet, as the watch below came racing out of the fo'cas'le beneath me.

"Now then! Now then! Now then!" shouted the Mate, as he charged up on to the fo'cas'le head.

"What's up?"

"It's something off the port bow, Sir," I said. "Running water! And then that sort of howl.... Your night-glasses," I suggested.

"Can't see a thing," he growled, as he stared away through the dark. "There's a sort of mist. Phoo! what a devil of a stink!"

"Look!" said someone down on the main-deck. "What's that?"

I saw it in the same instant, and caught the Mate's elbow.

"Look, Sir," I said. "There's a light there, about three points off the bow. It's moving."

The Mate was staring through his night-glasses, and suddenly he thrust them into my hands: —

"See if you can make it out," he said, and forthwith put his hands round his mouth, and bellowed into the night: — "Ahoy there! Ahoy there! Ahoy there!" his voice going out lost into the silence and darkness all around. But there came never a comprehensible answer, only all the time the infernal noise of a brook running out there on the sea, a thousand miles from any brook of earth; and away on the port bow, a vague shapeless shining.

I put the glasses to my eyes, and stared. The light was bigger and brighter, seen through the binoculars; but I could make nothing of it, only a dull, elongated shining, that moved vaguely in the darkness, apparently a hundred fathoms or so, away on the sea.

"Ahoy there! Ahoy there!" sung out the Mate again. Then, to the men below: — "Quiet there on the main-deck!"

There followed about a minute of intense stillness, during which we all listened; but there was no sound, except the constant noise of water running steadily.

I was watching the curious shining, and I saw it flick out suddenly at the Mate's shout. Then in a moment I saw three dull lights, one under the other, that flicked in and out intermittently.

"Here, give me the glasses!" said the Mate, and grabbed them from me.

He stared intensely for a moment; then swore, and turned to me: —

"What do you make of them?" he asked, abruptly.

"I don't know, Sir," I said. "I'm just puzzled. Perhaps it's electricity, or something of that sort."

"Oh hell!" he replied, and leant far out over the rail, staring, "Lord!" he said, for the second time, "what a stink!"

As he spoke, there came a most extraordinary thing; for there sounded a series of heavy reports out of the darkness, seeming in the silence, almost as loud as the sound of small cannon.

"They're shooting!" shouted a man on the main-deck, suddenly.

The Mate said nothing; only he sniffed violently at the night air. "By Gum!" he muttered, "what is it?"

I put my hand over my nose; for there was a terrible, charnel-like stench filling all the night about us.

"Take my glasses, Duprey," said the Mate, after a few minutes further watching. "Keep an eye over yonder. I'm going to call the Captain."

He pushed his way down the ladder, and hurried aft. About five minutes later, he returned forrard with the Captain and the Second and Third Mates, all in their shirts and trousers.

"Anything fresh, Duprey?" asked the Mate.

"No, Sir," I said, and handed him back his glasses. "The lights have gone again, and I think the mist is thicker. There's still the sound of running water out there."

The Captain and the three Mates stood some time along the port rail of the fo'cas'le head, watching through their night-glasses, and listening. Twice the Mate hailed; but there came no reply.

There was some talk, among the officers; and I gathered that the Captain was thinking of investigating.

"Clear one of the life-boats, Mr. Gelt," he said, at last. "The glass is steady; there'll be no wind for hours yet. Pick out a half a dozen men.

Take 'em out of either watch, if they want to come. I'll be back when I've got my coat."

"Away aft with you, Duprey, and some of you others," said the Mate. "Get the cover off the port life-boat, and bail her out."

"Aye, aye, Sir," I answered, and went away aft with the others.

We had the boat into the water within twenty minutes, which is good time for a wind-jammer, where boats are generally used as storage receptacles for odd gear.

I was one of the men told off to the boat, with two others from our watch, and one from the starboard.

The Captain came down the end of the main tops'l halyards into the boat, and the Third after him. The Third took the tiller, and gave orders to cast off.

We pulled out clear of our vessel, and the Skipper told us to lie on our oars for a moment while he took his bearings. He leant forward to listen, and we all did the same. The sound of the running water was quite distinct across the quietness; but it struck me as seeming not so loud as earlier.

I remember now, that I noticed how plain the mist had become — a sort of warm, wet mist; not a bit thick; but just enough to make the night very dark, and to be visible, eddying slowly in a thin vapour round the port side-light, looking like a red cloudiness swirling lazily through the red glow of the big lamp.

There was no other sound at this time, beyond the sound of the running water; and the Captain, after handing something to the Third Mate, gave the order to give-way.

I was rowing stroke, and close to the officers, and so was able to see dimly that the Captain had passed a heavy revolver over to the Third Mate.

"Ho!" I thought to myself, "so the Old Man's a notion there's really something dangerous over there."

I slipped a hand quickly behind me, and felt that my sheath knife was clear.

We pulled easily for about three or four minutes, with the sound of the water growing plainer somewhere ahead in the darkness; and astern of us, a vague red glowing through the night and vapour, showed where our vessel was lying.

We were rowing easily, when suddenly the bow-oar muttered "G'lord!" Immediately afterwards, there was a loud splashing in the water on his side of the boat.

"What's wrong in the bows, there?" asked the Skipper, sharply.

"There's somethin' in the water, Sir, messing round my oar," said the man.

I stopped rowing, and looked round. All the men did the same. There was a further sound of splashing, and the water was driven right over the boat in showers. Then the bow-oar called out: — "There's somethin' got a holt of my oar, Sir!"

I could tell the man was frightened; and I knew suddenly that a curious nervousness had come to me — a vague, uncomfortable dread, such as the memory of an ugly tale will bring, in a lonesome place. I believe every man in the boat had a similar feeling. It seemed to me in that moment, that a definite, muggy sort of silence was all round us, and this in spite of the sound of the splashing, and the strange noise of the running water somewhere ahead of us on the dark sea.

"It's let go the oar, Sir!" said the man.

Abruptly, as he spoke, there came the Captain's voice in a roar: — "Back water all!" he shouted. "Put some beef into it now! Back all! Back all!. . . Why the devil was no lantern put in the boat! Back now! Back! Back!"

We backed fiercely, with a will; for it was plain that the Old Man had some good reason to get the boat away pretty quickly. He was right, too; though, whether it was guess-work, or some kind of instinct that made him shout out at that moment, I don't know; only I am sure he could not have seen anything in that absolute darkness.

As I was saying, he was right in shouting to us to back; for we had not backed more than half a dozen fathoms, when there was a tremendous splash right ahead of us, as if a house had fallen into the sea; and a regular wave of sea-water came at us out of the darkness, throwing our bows up, and soaking us fore and aft.

"Good Lord!" I heard the Third Mate gasp out. "What the devil's that?"

"Back all! Back! Back!" the Captain sung out again.

After some moments, he had the tiller put over, and told us to pull. We gave way with a will, as you may think, and in a few minutes were alongside our own ship again.

"Now then, men," the Captain said, when we were safe aboard, "I'll not order any of you to come; but after the steward's served out a tot of grog each, those who are willing, can come with me, and we'll have another go at finding out what devil's work is going on over yonder."

He turned to the Mate, who had been asking questions: —

"Say, Mister," he said, "it's no sort of thing to let the boat go without a lamp aboard. Send a couple of the lads into the lamp locker, and pass out a couple of the anchor-lights, and that deck bull's-eye, you use at nights for clearing up the ropes."

He whipped round on the Third: — "Tell the steward to buck up with that grog, Mr. Andrews," he said, "and while you're there, pass out the axes from the rack in my cabin."

The grog came along a minute later; and then the Third Mate with three big axes from out the cabin rack.

"Now then, men," said the Skipper, as we took our tots off, "those who are coming with me, had better take an axe each from the Third Mate. They're mightly good weapons in any sort of trouble."

We all stepped forward, and he burst out laughing, slapping his thigh.

"That's the kind of thing I like!" he said. "Mr. Andrews, the axes won't go round. Pass out that old cutlass from the steward's pantry. It's a pretty hefty piece of iron!"

The old cutlass was brought, and the man who was short of an axe, collared it. By this time, two of the 'prentices had filled (at least we supposed they had filled them!) two of the ship's anchor-lights; also they had brought out the bull's-eye lamp we used when clearing up the ropes on a dark night. With the lights and the axes and the cutlass, we felt ready to face anything, and down we went again into the boat, with the Captain and the Third Mate after us.

"Lash one of the lamps to one of the boat-hooks, and rig it over the bows," ordered the Captain.

This was done, and in this way the light lit up the water for a couple of fathoms ahead of the boat; and made us feel less that something could come at us without our knowing. Then the painter was cast off, and we gave way again toward the sound of the running water, out there in the darkness.

I remember now that it struck me that our vessel had drifted a bit; for the sounds seemed farther away. The second anchor-light had been put in the stern of the boat, and the Third Mate kept it between his feet, while he steered. The Captain had the bull's-eye in his hand, and was pricking up the wick with his pocket-knife.

As we pulled, I took a glance or two over my shoulder; but could see nothing, except the lamp making a yellow halo in the mist round the boat's bows, as we forged ahead. Astern of us, on our quarter, I could see the dull red glow of our vessel's port light. That was all, and not a sound in all the sea, as you might say, except the roll of our oars in the rowlocks, and somewhere in the darkness ahead, that curious noise of water running steadily; now sounding, as I have said, fainter and seeming farther away.

"It's got my oar again, Sir!" exclaimed the man at the bow oar, suddenly, and jumped to his feet. He hove his oar up with a great splashing of water, into the air, and immediately something whirled and beat about in the yellow halo of light over the bows of the boat. There was a crash of breaking wood, and the boat-hook was broken. The lamp soused down into the sea, and was lost. Then in the darkness, there was a heavy splash, and a shout from the bow-oar: — "It's gone, Sir. It's loosed off the oar!"

"Vast pulling, all!" sung out the Skipper. Not that the order was necessary; for not a man was pulling. He had jumped up, and whipped a big revolver out of his coat pocket.

He had this in his right hand, and the bull's-eye in his left. He stepped forrard smartly over the oars from thwart to thwart, till he reached the bows, where he shone his light down into the water.

"My word!" he said. "Lord in Heaven! Saw anyone ever the like!"

And I doubt whether any man ever did see what we saw then; for the water was thick and living for yards round the boat with the hugest eels I ever saw before or after.

"Give way, Men," said the Skipper, after a minute. "Yon's no explanation of the almighty queer sounds out yonder we're hearing this night. Give way, lads!"

He stood right up in the bows of the boat, shining his bulls'-eye from side to side, and flashing it down on the water.

"Give way, lads!" he said again. "They don't like the light, that'll keep them from the oars. Give way steady now. Mr. Andrews, keep her dead on for the noise out yonder."

We pulled for some minutes, during which I felt my oar plucked at twice; but a flash of the Captain's lamp seemed sufficient to make the brutes loose hold.

The noise of the water running, appeared now quite near sounding. About this time, I had a sense again of an added sort of silence to all the natural quietness of the sea. And I had a return of the curious nervousness that had touched me before. I kept listening intensely, as if I expected to hear some other sound than the noise of the water. It came to me suddenly that I had the kind of feeling one has in the aisle of a large cathedral. There was a sort of echo in the night — an incredibly faint reduplicating of the noise of our oars.

"Hark!" I said, audibly; not realizing at first that I was speaking aloud. "There's an echo —"

"That's it!" the Captain cut in, sharply. "I thought I heard something rummy!"

. . . "I thought I heard something rummy," said a thin ghostly echo, out of the night. . . "thought I heard something rummy" . . . "heard something rummy." The words went muttering and whispering to and fro in the night about us, in a rather a horrible fashion.

"Good Lord!" said the Old Man, in a whisper.

We had all stopped rowing, and were staring about us into the thin mist that filled the night. The Skipper was standing with the bull's-eye lamp held over his head, circling the beam of light round from port to starboard, and back again.

Abruptly, as he did so, it came to me that the mist was thinner. The sound of the running water was very near; but it gave back no echo.

"The water doesn't echo, Sir," I said. "That's damn funny!"

"That's damn funny," came back at me, from the darkness to port and starboard, in a multitudinous muttering...."Damn funny!....funny... eey!"

"Give way!" said the Old Man, loudly. "I'll bottom this!"

"I'll bottom this. . .Bottom this. . .this!" The echo came back in a veritable rolling of unexpected sound. And then we had dipped our oars again, and the night was full of the reiterated rolling echoes of our row-locks.

Suddenly the echoes ceased, and there was, strangely, the sense of a great space about us, and in the same moment the sound of the water running appeared to be directly before us, but somehow up in the air.

"Vast rowing!" said the Captain, and we lay on our oars, staring round into the darkness ahead. The Old Man swung the beam of his lamp upwards, making circles with it in the night, and abruptly I saw something looming vaguely through the thinner-seeming mist.

"Look, Sir," I called to the Captain. "Quick, Sir, your light right above you! There's something up there!"

The Old Man flashed his lamp upwards, and found the thing I had seen. But it was too indistinct to make anything of, and even as he saw it, the darkness and mist seemed to wrap it about.

"Pull a couple of strokes, all!" said the Captain. "Stow your talk, there in the boat! . . . Again! . . . That'll do! Vast pulling!"

He was sending the beam of his lamp constantly across that part of the night where we had seen the thing, and suddenly I saw it again.

"There, Sir!" I said. "A little starboard with the light."

He flicked the light swiftly to the right, and immediately we all saw the thing plainly — a strangely-made mast, standing up there out of the mist, and looking like no spar I had ever seen.

It seemed now that the mist must lie pretty low on the sea in places; for the mast stood up out of it plainly for several fathoms; but, lower, it was hidden in the mist, which, I thought, seemed heavier now all round us; but thinner, as I have said, above.

"Ship ahoy!" sung out the Skipper, suddenly. "Ship ahoy, there!" But for some moments there came never a sound back to us except the constant noise of the water running, not a score yards away; and then, it seemed to me that a vague echo beat back at us out of the mist, oddly: — "Ahoy! Ahoy! Ahoy!"

"There's something hailing us, Sir," said the Third Mate.

Now, that "something" was significant. It showed the sort of feeling that was on us all.

"That's na ship's mast as ever I've seen!" I heard the man next to me mutter. "It's got a unnatcheral look."

"Ahoy there!" shouted the Skipper again, at the top of his voice. "Ahoy there!"

With the suddenness of a clap of thunder there burst out at us a vast, grunting: — oooaze; arrrr; arrrr; oooaze — a volume of sound so great that it seemed to make the loom of the oar in my hand vibrate.

"Good Lord!" said the Captain, and levelled his revolver into the mist; but he did not fire.

I had loosed one hand from my oar, and gripped my axe. I remember thinking that the Skipper's pistol wouldn't be much use against whatever thing made a noise like that.

"It wasn't ahead, Sir," said the Third Mate, abruptly, from where he sat and steered. "I think it came from somewhere over to starboard."

"Damn this mist!" said the Skipper. "Damn it! What a devil of a stink! Pass that other anchor-light forrard."

I reached for the lamp, and handed it to the next man, who passed it on.

"The other boat-hook," said the Skipper; and when he'd got it, he lashed the lamp to the hook end, and then lashed the whole arrangement upright in the bows, so that the lamp was well above his head.

"Now," he said. "Give way gently! And stand by to back-water, if I tell you.... Watch my hand, Mister," he added to the Third Mate. "Steer as I tell you."

We rowed a dozen slow strokes, and with every stroke, I took a look over my shoulder. The Captain was leaning forward under the big lamp, with the bull's-eye in one hand and his revolver in the other. He kept flashing the beam of the lantern up into the night.

"Good Lord!" he said, suddenly. "Vast pulling."

We stopped, and I slewed round on the thwart, and stared.

He was standing up under the glow of the anchor-light, and shining the bull's-eye up at a great mass that loomed dully through the mist. As he flicked the light to and fro over the great bulk, I realized that the boat was within some three or four fathoms of the hull of a vessel.

"Pull another stroke," the Skipper said, in a quiet voice, after a few minutes of silence. "Gently now! Gently! . . . Vast pulling!"

I slewed round again on my thwart and stared. I could see part of the thing quite distinctly now, and more of it, as I followed the beam of the Captain's lantern. She was a vessel right enough; but such a vessel as I had never seen. She was extraordinarily high out of the water, and seemed very short, and rose up into a queer mass at one end. But what puzzled me more, I think, than anything else, was the queer look of her sides, down which water was streaming all the time.

"That explains the sound of the water running," I thought to myself; "but what on earth is she built of?"

You will understand a little of my bewildered feelings, when I tell you that as the beam of the Captain's lamp shone on the side of this queer vessel, it showed stone everywhere — as if she were built out of stone. I never felt so dumb-founded in my life.

"She's stone, Cap'n" I said. "Look at her, Sir!"

I realised, as I spoke, a certain horribleness, of the unnatural.... A stone ship, floating out there in the night in the midst of the lonely Atlantic!

"She's stone," I said again, in that absurd way in which one reiterates, when one is bewildered.

"Look at the slime on her!" muttered the man next but one forrard of me. "She's a proper Davy Jones ship. By gum! she stinks like a corpse!"

"Ship ahoy!" roared the Skipper, at the top of his voice. "Ship ahoy! Ship ahoy!"

His shout beat back at us, in a curious, dank, yet metallic, echo, something the way one's voice sounds in an old disused quarry.

"There's no one aboard there, Sir," said the Third Mate. "Shall I put the boat alongside?"

"Yes, shove her up, Mister," said the Old Man. "I'll bottom this business. Pull a couple of strokes, aft there! In bow, and stand by to fend off."

The Third Mate laid the boat alongside, and we unshipped our oars.

Then, I leant forward over the side of the boat, and pressed the flat of my hand upon the stark side of the ship. The water that ran down her side, sprayed out over my hand and wrist in a cataract; but I did not think about being wet, for my hand was pressed solid upon stone.... I pulled my hand back with a queer feeling.

"She's stone, right enough, Sir," I said to the Captain.

"We'll soon see what she is," he said. "Shove your oar up against her side, and shin up. We'll pass the lamp up to you as soon as you're aboard. Shove your axe in the back of your belt. I'll cover you with my gun, till you're aboard."

"Aye, aye, Sir," I said; though I felt a bit funny at the thought of having to be the first aboard that damn rummy craft.

I put my oar upright against her side, and took a spring up from the thwart, and in a moment I was grabbing over my head for her rail, with every rag of me soaked through with the water that was streaming down her, and spraying out over the oar and me.

I got a firm grip of the rail, and hoisted my head high enough to look over; but I could see nothing .... what with the darkness, and the water in my eyes.

I knew it was no time for going slow, if there were danger aboard; so I went in over that rail in one spring, my boots coming down with a horrible, ringing, hollow, stony sound on her decks. I whipped the water out of my eyes and the axe out of my belt, all in the same moment; then I took a good stare fore and aft; but it was too dark to see anything.

"Come along, Duprey!" shouted the Skipper. "Collar the lamp."

I leant out sideways over the rail, and grabbed for the lamp with my left hand, keeping the axe ready in my right, and staring inboard; for I tell you, I was just mortally afraid in that moment of what might be aboard of her.

I felt the lamp-ring with my left hand, and gripped it. Then I switched it aboard, and turned fair and square to see where I'd gotten.

Now, you never saw such a packet as that, not in a hundred years, nor yet two hundred, I should think. She'd got a rum little main-deck, about forty feet long, and then came a step about two feet high, and another bit of a deck, with a little house on it.

That was the after end of her; and more I couldn't see, because the light of my lamp went no farther, except to show me vaguely the big, cocked-up stern of her, going up into the darkness. I never saw a vessel made like her; not even in an old picture of old-time ships.

Forrard of me, was her mast — a big lump of a stick it was too, for her size. And here was another amazing thing, the mast of her looked just solid stone.

"Funny, isn't she, Duprey?" said the Skipper's voice at my back, and

I came round on him with a jump.

"Yes," I said. "I'm puzzled. Aren't you, Sir?"

"Well," he said, "I am. If we were like the shellbacks they talk of in books, we'd be crossing ourselves. But, personally, give me a good heavy Colt, or the hefty chunk of steel you're cuddling."

He turned from me, and put his head over the rail.

"Pass up the painter, Jales," he said, to the bow-oar. Then to the Third Mate: —

"Bring 'em all up, Mister. If there's going to be anything rummy, we may as well make a picnic party of the lot.... Hitch that painter round the cleet yonder, Duprey," he added to me. "It looks good solid stone! . . . That's right. Come along."

He swung the thin beam of his lantern fore and aft, and then forrard again.

"Lord!" he said. "Look at that mast. It's stone. Give it a whack with the back of your axe, man; only remember she's apparently a bit of an old-timer! So go gently."

I took my axe short, and tapped the mast, and it rang dull, and solid, like a stone pillar, I struck it again, harder, and a sharp flake of stone flew past my cheek. The Skipper thrust his lantern close up to where I'd struck the mast.

"By George," he said, "she's absolute a stone ship — solid stone, afloat here out of Eternity, in the middle of the wide Atlantic.... Why! She must weigh a thousand tons more than she's buoyancy to carry. It's just impossible.... It's —"

He turned his head quickly, at a sound in the darkness along the decks. He flashed his light that way, across the after decks; but we could see nothing

"Get a move on you in the boat!" he said sharply, stepping to the rail and looking down. "For once I'd really prefer a little more of your company...." He came round like a flash. "Duprey, what was that?" he asked in a low voice.

"I certainly heard something, Sir," I said. "I wish the others would hurry. By Jove! Look! What's that —"

"Where?" he said, and sent the beam of his lamp to where I pointed with my axe.

"There's nothing," he said, after circling the light all over the deck. "Don't go imagining things. There's enough solid unnatural fact here, without trying to add to it."

There came the splash and thud of feet behind, as the first of the men came up over the side, and jumped clumsily into the lee scuppers, which had water in them. You see she had a cant to that side, and I supposed the water had collected there.

The rest of the men followed, and then the Third Mate. That made six men of us, all well armed; and I felt a bit more comfortable, as you can think.

"Hold up that lamp of yours, Duprey, and lead the way," said the Skipper. "You're getting the post of honour this trip!"

"Aye, aye, Sir," I said, and stepped forward, holding up the lamp in my left hand, and carrying my axe half way down the haft, in my right.

"We'll try aft, first," said the Captain, and led the way himself, flashing the bull's-eye to and fro. At the raised portion of the deck, he stopped.

"Now," he said, in his queer way, "let's have a look at this.... Tap it with your axe, Duprey.... Ah!" he added, as I hit it with the back of my axe. "That's what we call stone at home, right enough. She's just as rum as anything I've seen while I've been fishing. We'll go on aft and have a peep into the deck-house. Keep your axes handy, men."

We walked slowly up to the curious little house, the deck rising to it with quite a slope. At the foreside of the little deck-house, the Captain pulled up, and shone his bull's-eye down at the deck. I saw that he was looking at what was plainly the stump of the after mast. He stepped closer to it, and kicked it with his foot; and it gave out the same dull, solid note that the foremast had done. It was obviously a chunk of stone.

I held up my lamp so that I could see the upper part of the house more clearly. The fore-part had two square window-spaces in it; but there was no glass in either of them; and the blank darkness within the queer little place, just seemed to stare out at us.

And then I saw something suddenly . . . a great shaggy head of red hair was rising slowly into sight, through the port window, the one nearest to us.

"My God! What's that, Cap'n?" I called out. But it was gone, even as I spoke.

"What?" he asked, jumping at the way I had sung out.

"At the port window, Sir," I said. "A great red-haired head. It came right up to the window-place; and then it went in a moment."

The Skipper stepped right up to the little dark window, and pushed his lantern through into the blackness. He flashed a light round; then withdrew the lantern.

"Bosh, man!" he said. "That's twice you've got fancying things. Ease up your nerves a bit!"

"I did see it!" I said, almost angrily. "It was like a great red-haired head...."

"Stow it, Duprey!" he said, though not sneeringly. "The house is absolutely empty. Come round to the door, if the Infernal Masons that built her, went in for doors! Then you'll see for yourself. All the same, keep your axes ready, lads. I've a notion there's something pretty queer aboard here."

We went up round the after-end of the little house, and here we saw what appeared to be a door.

The Skipper felt at the queer, odd-shapen handle, and pushed at the door; but it had stuck fast.

"Here, one of you!" he said, stepping back. "Have a whack at this with your axe. Better use the back."

One of the men stepped forward, and stood away to give him room. As his axe struck, the door went to pieces with exactly the same sound that a thin slab of stone would make, when broken.

"Stone!" I heard the Captain mutter, under his breath. "By Gum! What is she?"

I did not wait for the Skipper. He had put me a bit on edge, and I stepped bang in through the open doorway, with the lamp high, and holding my axe short and ready; but there was nothing in the place, save a stone seat running all round, except where the doorway opened on to the deck.

"Find your red-haired monster?" asked the Skipper, at my elbow.

I said nothing. I was suddenly aware that he was all on the jump with some inexplicable fear. I saw his glance going everywhere about him. And then his eye caught mine, and he saw that I realised. He was a man almost callous to fear, that is the fear of danger in what I might call any normal sea-faring shape. And this palpable nerviness affected me tremendously. He was obviously doing his best to throttle it; and trying all he knew to hide it. I had a sudden warmth of understanding for him, and dreaded lest the men should realise his state. Funny that I should be able at that moment to be aware of anything but my own bewildered fear and expectancy of intruding upon something monstrous at any instant. Yet I describe exactly my feelings, as I stood there in the house.

"Shall we try below, Sir?" I said, and turned to where a flight of stone steps led down into an utter blackness, out which rose a strange, dank scent of the sea. . . an imponderable mixture of brine and darkness.

"The worthy Duprey leads the van!" said the Skipper; but I felt no irritation now. I knew that he must cover his fright, until he had got control again; and I think he felt, somehow, that I was backing him up. I remember now that I went down those stairs into that unknowable and ancient cabin, as much aware in that moment of the Captain's state, as of that extraordinary thing I had just seen at the little window, or of my own half-funk of what we might see any moment.

The Captain was at my shoulder, as I went, and behind him came the Third Mate, and then the men, all in single file; for the stairs were narrow.

I counted seven steps down, and then my foot splashed into water on the eighth. I held the lamp low and stared. I had caught no glimpse of a reflection, and I saw now that this was owing to a curious, dull, greyish scum that lay thinly on the water, seeming to match the colour of the stone which composed the steps and bulkheads.

"Stop!" I said. "I'm in water!"

I let my foot down slowly, and got the next step. Then sounded with my axe, and found the floor at the bottom. I stepped down and stood up to my thighs in water.

"It's all right, Sir," I said, suddenly whispering. I held my lamp up, and glanced quickly about me.

"It's not deep. There's two doors here...."

I whirled my axe up as I spoke; for suddenly, I had realised that one of the doors was open a little. It seemed to move, as I stared, and I could have imagined that a vague undulation ran towards me, across the dull scum-covered water.

"The door's opening!" I said, aloud, with a sudden sick feeling. "Look out!"

I backed from the door, staring; but nothing came. And abruptly, I had control of myself; for I realised that the door was not moving. It had not moved at all. It was simply ajar.

"It's all right, sir," I said. "It's not opening."

I stepped forward again a pace towards the doors, as the Skipper and the Third Mate came down with a jump, splashing water all over me.

The Captain still had the "nerves," on him, as I think I could feel, even then; but he hid it well.

"Try the door, Mister. I've jumped my damn lamp out!" he growled to the Third Mate; who pushed at the door on my right; but it would not open beyond the nine or ten inches it was fixed ajar.

"There's this one here, Sir," I whispered, and held my lantern up to the closed door that lay on my left.

"Try it," said the Skipper, in an undertone. We did so, but it also was fixed. I whirled my axe suddenly, and struck the door heavily in the centre of the main panel, and the whole thing crashed into flinders of stone, that went with hollow sounding splashes into the darkness beyond.

"Goodness!" said the Skipper, in a startled voice; for my action had been so instant and unexpected. He covered his lapse, in a moment, by the warning: —

"Look out for bad air!" But I was already inside with the lamp, and holding my axe handily. There was no bad air; for right across from me, was a split clean through the ship's side, that I could have put my two arms through, just above the level of the scummy water.

The place I had broken into, was a cabin, of a kind; but seemed strange and dank, and too narrow to breathe in; and wherever I turned, I saw stone. The Third Mate and the Skipper gave simultaneous expressions of disgust at the wet dismalness of the place.

"It's all of stone," I said, and brought my axe hard against the front of a sort of squat cabinet, which was built into the after bulkheads. It caved in, with a crash of splintered stone.

"Empty!" I said, and turned instantly away.

The Skipper and the Third Mate, with the men who were now peering in at the door, crowded out; and in that moment, I pushed my axe under my arm, and thrust my hand into the burst stone-chest. Twice I did this, with almost the speed of lightning, and shoved what I had seen, into the side-pocket of my coat. Then, I was following the others; and not one of them had noticed a thing. As for me, I was quivering with excitement, so that my knees shook; for I had caught the unmistakable gleam of gems; and had grabbed for them in that one swift instant.

I wonder whether anyone can realise what I felt in that moment. I knew that, if my guess were right, I had snatched the power in that one miraculous moment, that would lift me from the weary life of a common shellback, to the life of ease that had been mine during my early years. I tell you, in that instant, as I staggered almost blindly out of that dark little apartment, I had no thought of any horror that might be held in that incredible vessel, out there afloat on the wide Atlantic.

I was full of one blinding thought, that possibly I was rich! And I wanted to get somewhere by myself as soon as possible, to see whether I was right. Also, if I could, I meant to get back to that strange cabinet of stone, if the chance came; for I knew that the two handfuls I had grabbed, had left a lot behind.

Only, whatever I did, I must let no one guess; for then I should probably lose everything, or have but an infinitesimal share doled out to me, of the wealth that I believed to be in those glittering things there in the side-pocket of my coat.

I began immediately to wonder what other treasures there might be aboard; and then, abruptly, I realised that the Captain was speaking to me:

"The light, Duprey, damn you!" he was saying, angrily, in a low tone. "What's the matter with you! Hold it up."

I pulled myself together, and shoved the lamp above my head. One of the men was swinging his axe, to beat in the door that seemed to have stood so eternally ajar; and the rest were standing back, to give him room. Crash! went the axe, and half the door fell inward, in a shower of broken stone, making dismal splashes in the darkness. The man struck again, and the rest of the door fell away, with a sullen slump into the water.

"The lamp," muttered the Captain. But I had hold of myself once more, and I was stepping forward slowly through the thigh-deep water, even before he spoke.

I went a couple of paces in through the black gape of the doorway, and then stopped and held the lamp so as to get a view of the place. As I did so, I remember how the intense silence struck home on me. Every man of us must surely have been holding his breath; and there must have been some heavy quality, either in the water, or in the scum that floated on it, that kept it from rippling against the sides of the bulkheads, with the movements we had made.

At first, as I held the lamp (which was burning badly), I could not get its position right to show me anything, except that I was in a very large cabin for so small a vessel. Then I saw that a table ran along the centre, and the top of it was no more than a few inches above the water. On each side of it, there rose the backs of what were evidently two rows of massive, olden looking chairs. At the far end of the table, there was a huge, immobile, humped something.

I stared at this for several moments; then I took three slow steps forward, and stopped again; for the thing resolved itself, under the light from the lamp, into the figure of an enormous man, seated at the end of the table, his face bowed forward upon his arms. I was amazed, and thrilling abruptly with new fears and vague impossible thoughts. Without moving a step, I held the light nearer at arm's length.... The man was of stone, like everything in that extraordinary ship.

"That foot!" said the Captain's voice, suddenly cracking. "Look at that foot!" His voice sounded amazingly startling and hollow in that silence, and the words seemed to come back sharply at me from the vaguely seen bulkheads.

I whipped my light to starboard, and saw what he meant — a huge human foot was sticking up out of the water, on the right hand of the table. It was enormous. I have never seen so vast a foot. And it also was of stone.

And then, as I stared, I saw that there was a great head above the water, over by the bulkhead.

"I've gone mad!" I said, out loud, as I saw something else, more incredible.

"My God! Look at the hair on the head!" said the Captain.... "It's growing!" he called out once more.

I was looking. On the great head, there was becoming visible a huge mass of red hair, that was surely and unmistakably rising up, as we watched it.

"It's what I saw at the window!" I said. "It's what I saw at the window! I told you I saw it!"

"Come out of that, Duprey," said the Third Mate, quietly.

"Let's get out of here!" muttered one of the men. Two or three of them called out the same thing; and then, in a moment, they began a mad rush up the stairway.

I stood dumb, where I was. The hair rose up in a horrible living fashion on the great head, waving and moving. It rippled down over the forehead, and spread abruptly over the whole gargantuan stone face, hiding the features completely. Suddenly, I swore at the thing madly, and I hove my axe at it. Then I was backing crazily for the door, slumping the scum as high as the deck beams, in my fierce haste. I reached the stairs, and caught at the stone rail, that was modelled like a rope; and so hove myself up out of the water. I reached the deck-house, where I had seen the great head of hair. I jumped through the doorway, out on to the decks, and felt the night air sweet on my face.... Goodness! I ran forward along the decks. There was a Babel of shouting in the waist of the ship, and a thudding of feet running. Some of the men were singing out, to get into the boat; but the Third Mate was shouting that they must wait for me.

"He's coming," called someone. And then I was among them.

"Turn that lamp up, you idiot," said the Captain's voice. "This is just where we want light!"

I glanced down, and realised that my lamp was almost out. I turned it up, and it flared, and began again to dwindle.

"Those damned boys never filled it," I said. "They deserve their necks breaking."

The men were literally tumbling over the side, and the Skipper was hurrying them.

"Down with you into the boat," he said to me. "Give me the lamp. I'll pass it down. Get a move on you!"

The Captain had evidently got his nerve back again. This was more like the man I knew. I handed him the lamp, and went over the side. All the rest had now gone, and the Third Mate was already in the stern, waiting.

As I landed on the thwart, there was a sudden strange noise from aboard the ship — a sound, as if some stone object were trundling down the sloping decks, from aft. In that one moment, I got what you might truly call the "horrors." I seemed suddenly able to believe incredible possibilities.

"The stone men!" I shouted. "Jump, Captain! Jump! Jump!" The vessel seemed to roll oddly.

Abruptly, the Captain yelled out something, that not one of us in the boat understood. There followed a succession of tremendous sounds, aboard the ship, and I saw his shadow swing out huge against the thin mist, as he turned suddenly with the lamp. He fired twice with his revolver.

"The hair!" I shouted. "Look at the hair!"

We all saw it — the great head of red hair that we had seen grow visibly on the monstrous stone head, below in the cabin. It rose above the rail, and there was a moment of intense stillness, in which I heard the Captain gasping. The Third Mate fired six times at the thing, and I found myself fixing an oar up against the side of that abominable vessel, to get aboard.

As I did so, there came one appalling crash, that shook the stone ship fore and aft, and she began to cant up, and my oar slipped and fell into the boat. Then the Captain's voice screamed something in a choking fashion above us. The ship lurched forward and paused. Then another crash came, and she rocked over towards us; then away from us again. The movement away from us continued, and the round of the vessel's bottom showed, vaguely. There was a smashing of glass above us, and the dim glow of light aboard vanished. Then the vessel fell clean from us, with a giant splash. A huge wave came at us, out of the night, and half filled the boat.

The boat nearly capsized, then righted and presently steadied.

"Captain!" shouted the Third Mate. "Captain!" But there came never a sound; only presently, out of all the night, a strange murmuring of waters.

"Captain!" he shouted once more; but his voice just went lost and remote into the darkness.

"She's foundered!" I said.

"Out oars," sung out the Third. "Put your backs into it. Don't stop to bail!"

For half an hour we circled the spot slowly. But the strange vessel had indeed foundered and gone down into the mystery of the deep sea, with her mysteries.

Finally we put about, and returned to the *Alfred Jessop*.

Now, I want you to realize that what I am telling you is a plain and simple tale of fact. This is no fairy tale, and I've not done yet; and I think this yarn should prove to you that some mighty strange things do happen at sea, and always will while the world lasts. It's the home of all mysteries; for it's the one place that is really difficult for humans to investigate. Now just listen: —

The Mate had kept the bell going, from time to time, and so we came back pretty quickly, having as we came, a strange repetition of the echo-ey reduplication of our oar-sounds; but we never spoke a word; for not one of us wanted to hear those beastly echoes again, after what we had just gone through. I think we all had a feeling that there was something a bit hellish aboard that night.

We got aboard, and the Third explained to the Mate what had happened; but he would hardly believe the yarn. However, there was nothing to do, but wait for daylight; so we were told to keep about the deck, and keep our eyes and ears open.

One thing the Mate did show he was more impressed by our yarn than he would admit. He had all the ships' lanterns lashed up round the decks, to the sheerpoles; and he never told us to give up either the axes or cutlass.

It was while we were keeping about the decks, that I took the chance to have a look at what I had grabbed. I tell you, what I found, made me nearly forget the Skipper, and all the rummy things that had happened. I had twenty-six stones in my pocket and four of them were diamonds, respectively 9, 11, 13 1/2 and 17 carats in weight, uncut, that is. I know quite something about diamonds. I'm not going to tell you how I learnt what I know; but I would not have taken a thousand pounds for the four, as they lay there, in my hand. There was also a big, dull stone, that looked red inside. I'd have dumped it over the side, I thought so little of it; only, I argued that it must be something, or it would never have been among that lot. Lord! but I little knew what I'd got; not then. Why, the thing was as big as a fair-sized walnut. You may think it funny that I thought of the four diamonds first; but you see, I know diamonds when I see them. They're things I understand; but I never saw a ruby, in the rough, before or since. Good Lord! And to think I'd have thought nothing of heaving it over the side!

You see, a lot of the stones were not anything much; that is, not in the modern market. There were two big topazes, and several onyx and corelians — nothing much. There were five hammered slugs of gold about two ounces each they would be. And then a prize — one winking green devil of an emerald. You're got to know an emerald to look for the "eye" of it, in the rough; but it is there — the eye of some hidden devil staring up at you. Yes, I'd seen an emerald before, and I knew I held a lot of money in that one stone alone.

And then I remembered what I'd missed, and cursed myself for not grabbing a third time. But that feeling lasted only a moment. I thought of the beastly part that had been the Skipper's share; while there I stood safe under one of the lamps, with a fortune in my hands. And then, abruptly, as you can understand, my mind was filled with the crazy wonder and bewilderment of what had happened. I felt how absurdly ineffectual my imagination was to comprehend anything understandable out of it all, except that the Captain had certainly gone, and I had just as certainly had a piece of impossible luck.

Often, during that time of waiting, I stopped to take a look at the things I had in my pocket; always careful that no one about the decks should come near me, to see what I was looking at.

Suddenly the Mate's voice came sharp along the decks: —

"Call the doctor, one of you," he said. "Tell him to get the fire in and the coffee made."

"Aye Sir," said one of the men; and I realized that the dawn was growing vaguely over the sea.

Half an hour later, the "doctor" shoved his head out of the galley doorway, and sung out that coffee was ready.

The watch below turned out, and had theirs with the watch on deck, all sitting along the spar that lay under the port rail.

As the daylight grew, we kept a constant watch over the side; but even now we could see nothing; for the thin mist still hung low on the sea.

"Hear that?" said one of the men, suddenly. And, indeed, the sound must have been plain for a half a mile round.

"Ooaaze, ooaaze, arr, arrrr, oooaze —"

"By George!" said Tallett, one of the other watch; "that's a beastly sort of thing to hear."

"Look!" I said. "What's that out yonder?"

The mist was thinning under the effect of the rising sun, and tremendous shapes seemed to stand towering half-seen, away to port. A few minutes passed, while we stared. Then, suddenly, we heard the Mate's voice —

"All hands on deck!" he was shouting, along the decks.

I ran aft a few steps.

"Both watches are out, Sir," I called.

"Very good!" said the Mate. "Keep handy all of you. Some of you have got the axes. The rest had better take a caps-n-bar each, and stand-by till I find what this devilment is, out yonder."

"Aye, aye,Sir," I said, and turned forrard. But there was no need to pass on the Mate's orders; for the men had heard, and there was a rush for the capstanbars, which are a pretty hefty kind of cudgel, as any sail-orman knows. We lined the rail again, and stared away to port.

"Look out, you sea-divvils," shouted Timothy Galt, a huge Irishman, waving his bar excitedly, and peering over the rail into the mist, which was steadily thinning, as the day grew.

Abruptly there was a simultaneous cry — "*Rocks!*" shouted every-one.

I never saw such a sight. As at last the mist thinned, we could see them. All the sea to port was literally cut about with far-reaching reefs of rock. In places the reefs lay just submerged; but in others they rose into extraordinary and fantastic rock-spires, and arches, and islands of jagged rock.

"Jehosaphat!" I heard the Third Mate shout. "Look at that, Mister! Look at that! Lord! how did we take the boat through that, without stov-ing her!"

Everthing was so still for the moment, with all the men just staring and amazed, that I could hear every word come along the decks.

"There's sure been a submarine earthquake somewhere," I heard the First Mate. "The bottom of the sea's just riz up here, quiet and gentle, during the night; and God's mercy we aren't now a-top of one of those ornaments out there."

And then, you know, I saw it all. Everything that had looked mad and impossible, began to be natural; though it was, none the less, all amazing and wonderful.

There had been during the night, a slow lifting of the sea-bottom, owing to some action of the Internal Pressures. The rocks had risen so gently that they had made never a sound; and the stone ship had risen with them out of the deep sea. She had evidently lain on one of the submerged reefs, and so had seemed to us to be just afloat in the sea. And she accounted for the water we heard running. She was naturally bung full, as you might say, and took longer to shed the water than she did to rise. She had probably some biggish holes in her bottom. I began to get my "soundings" a bit, as I might call it in sailor talk. The natural wonders of the sea beat all made-up yarns that ever were!

The Mate sung out to us to man the boat again, and told the Third Mate to take her out to where we lost the Skipper, and have a final look round, in case there might be any chance to find the Old Man's body anywhere about.

"Keep a man in the bows to look out for sunk rocks, Mister," the Mate told the Third, as we pulled off. "Go slow. There'll be no wind yet awhile. See if you can fix up what made those noises, while you're looking round."

We pulled right across about thirty fathoms of clear water, and in a minute we were between two great arches of rock. It was then I realized that the reduplicating of our oar-roll was the echo from these on each side of us. Even in the sunlight, it was queer to hear again that same strange cathedral echoey sound that we had heard in the dark.

We passed under the huge arches, all hung with deep-sea slime. And presently we were heading straight for a gap, where two low reefs swept in to the apex of a huge horseshoe. We pulled for about three minutes, and then the Third gave the word to vast pulling.

"Take the boat-hook, Duprey," he said, "and go forrard, and see we don't hit anything."

"Aye, aye, Sir," I said, and drew in my oar.

"Give way again gently!" said the Third; and the boat moved forward for another thirty or forty yards.

"We're right on to a reef, Sir," I said, presently, as I stared down over the bows. I sounded with the boat-hook. "There's about three feet of water, Sir," I told him.

"Vast pulling," ordered the Third. "I reckon we are right over the rock, where we found that rum packet last night." He leant over the side, and stared down.

"There's a stone cannon on the rock, right under the bows of the boat," I said. Immediately afterwards I shouted —

"There's the hair, Sir! There's the hair! It's on the reef. There's two! There's three! There's one on the cannon!"

"All right! All right, Duprey! Keep cool," said the Third Mate. "I can see them. You're enough intelligence not to be superstitious now the whole thing's explained. They're some kind of big hairy sea-caterpillar. Prod one with your boat-hook."

I did so; a little ashamed of my sudden bewilderment. The thing whipped round like a tiger, at the boat-hook. It lapped itself round and round the boat-hook, while the hind portions of it kept gripped to the rock, and I could no more pull the boat-hook from its grip, than fly; though I pulled till I sweated.

"Take the point of your cutlass to it, Varley," said the Third Mate. "Jab it through."

The bow-oar did so, and the brute loosed the boat-hook, and curled up round a chunk of rock, looking like a great ball of red hair.

I drew the boat-hook up, and examined it.

"Goodness!" I said. "That's what killed the Old Man — one of those things! Look at all those marks in the wood, where it's gripped it with about a hundred legs."

I passed the boat-hook aft to the Third Mate to look at.

"They're about as dangerous as they can be, Sir, I reckon," I told him.

"Makes you think of African centipedes, only these are big and strong enough to kill an elephant, I should think."

"Don't lean all on one side of the boat!" shouted the Third Mate, as the men stared over. "Get back to your places. Give way, there! . . . Keep a good look-out for any signs of the ship or the Captain, Duprey."

For nearly an hour, we pulled to and fro over the reef; but we never saw either the stone ship or the Old Man again. The queer craft must have rolled off into the profound depths that lay on each side of the reef.

As I leant over the bows, staring down all that long while at the submerged rocks, I was able to understand almost everything, except the various extraordinary noises.

The cannon made it unmistakably clear that the ship which had been hove up from the sea-bottom, with the rising of the reef, had been originally a normal enough wooden vessel of a time far removed from our own. At the sea-bottom, she had evidently undergone some natural mineralizing process, and this explained her stony appearance. The stone men had been evidently humans who had been drowned in her cabin, and their swollen tissues had been subjected to the same natural process, which, however, had also deposited heavy encrustations upon them, so that their size, when compared with the normal, was prodigious.

The mystery of the hair, I had already discovered; but there remained, among other things, the tremendous bangs we had heard. These were, possibly, explained later, while we were making a final examination of the rocks to the westward, prior to returning to our ship. Here we discovered the burst and swollen bodies of several extraordinary deep-sea creatures, of the eel variety. They must have had a girth, in life, of many feet, and one that we measured roughly with an oar, must have been quite forty feet long. They had, apparently, burst on being lifted from the tremendous pressure of the deep sea, into the light air pressure above water, and hence might account for the loud reports we had heard; though, personally, I incline to think these loud bangs were more probably caused by the splitting of the rocks under new stresses.

As for the roaring sounds, I can only conclude that they were caused by a peculiar species of grampus-like fish, of enormous size, which we found dead and hugely distended on one of the rocky masses. This fish must have weighed at least four or five tons, and when prodded with a heavy oar, there came from its peculiar snout-shaped mouth, a low, hoarse sound, like a weak imitation of the tremendous sounds we had heard during the past night.

Regarding the apparently carved handrail, like a rope up the side of the cabin stairs, I realize that this had undoubtedly been actual rope at one time.

Recalling the heavy, trundling sounds aboard, just after I climbed down into the boat, I can only suppose that these were made by some stone object, possibly a fossilized gun-carriage, rolling down the decks, as the ship began to slip off the rocks, and bows sank lower in the water.

The varying lights must have been the strongly phosphorescent bodies of some of the deep-sea creatures, moving about on the upheaved reefs. As for the giant splash that occurred in the darkness ahead of the boat, this must have been due to some large portion of heaved-up rock, over-balancing and rolling back into the sea.

No one aboard ever learnt about the jewels. I took care of that! I sold the ruby badly, so I've heard since; but I do not grumble even now. Twenty-three thousand pounds I had for it alone, from a merchant in London. I learned afterwards he made double that on it; but I don't spoil my pleasure by grumbling. I wonder often how the stones and things came where I found them; but she carried guns, as I've told, I think; and there's rum doings happen at sea; yes, by George!

The smell — oh that I guess was due to heaving all that deep-sea slime up for human noses to smell at.

This yarn is, of course, known in nautical circles, and was briefly mentioned in the old *Nautical Mercury* of 1879. The series of volcanic reefs (which disappeared in 1883) were charted under the name of the "Alfred Jessop Shoals and Reefs"; being named after our Captain who discovered them and lost his life on them.

# THE THING IN THE WEEDS

THIS is an extraordinary tale. We had come up from the Cape, and owing to the Trades heading us more than usual, we had made some hundreds of miles more westing than I ever did before or since.

I remember the particular night of the happening perfectly. I suppose what occurred stamped it solid into my m7emory, with a thousand little details that, in the ordinary way, I should never have remembered an hour. And, of course, we talked it over so often among ourselves that this, no doubt, helped to fix it all past any forgetting.

I remember the mate and I had been pacing the weather side of the poop and discussing various old shellbacks' superstitions. I was third mate, and it was between four and five bells in the first watch, i.e. between ten and half-past. Suddenly he stopped in his walk and lifted his head and sniffed several times.

"My word, mister," he said, "there's a rum kind of stink somewhere about. Don't you smell it?"

I sniffed once or twice at the light airs that were coming in on the beam; then I walked to the rail and leaned over, smelling again at the slight breeze. And abruptly I got a whiff of it, faint and sickly, yet vaguely suggestive of something I had once smelt before.

"I can smell something, Mr. Lammart," I said. "I could almost give it name; and yet somehow I can't." I stared away into the dark to windward. "What do you seem to smell?" I asked him.

"I can't smell anything now," he replied, coming over and standing beside me. "It's gone again. No! By Jove! there it is again. My goodness! Phew!"

The smell was all about us now, filling the night air. It had still that indefinable familiarity about it, and yet it was curiously strange, and, more than anything else, it was certainly simply beastly.

The stench grew stronger, and presently the mate asked me to go for'ard and see whether the look-out man noticed anything. When I reached the break of the fo'c's'le head I called up to the man, to know whether he smelled anything.

"Smell anythin', sir?" he sang out. "Jumpin' larks! I sh'u'd think I do. I'm fair p'isoned with it."

I ran up the weather steps and stood beside him. The smell was certainly very plain up there, and after savouring it for a few moments I asked him whether he thought it might be a dead whale. But he was very emphatic that this could not be the case, for, as he said, he had been nearly fifteen years in whaling ships, and knew the smell of a dead whale, "like as you would the smell of bad whiskey, sir," as he put it. "'Tain't no whale yon, but the Lord He knows what 'tis. I'm thinking it's Davy Jones come up for a breather."

I stayed with him some minutes, staring out into the darkness, but could see nothing; for, even had there been something big close to us, I doubt whether I could have seen it, so black a night it was, without a visible star, and with a vague, dull haze breeding an indistinctness all about the ship.

I returned to the mate and reported that the look-out complained of the smell, but that neither he nor I had been able to see anything in the darkness to account for it.

By this time the queer, disgusting odour seemed to be in all the air about us, and the mate told me to go below and shut all the ports, so as to keep the beastly smell out of the cabins and the saloon.

When I returned he suggested that we should shut the companion doors, and after that we commenced to pace the poop again, discussing the extraordinary smell, and stopping from time to time to stare through our night-glasses out into the night about the ship.

"I'll tell you what it smells like, mister," the mate remarked once, "and that's like a mighty old derelict I once went aboard in the North Atlantic. She was a proper old-timer, an' she gave us all the creeps. There was just this funny, dank, rummy sort of century-old bilge-water and dead men an' seaweed. I can't stop thinkin' we're nigh some lonesome old packet out there; an' a good thing we've not much way on us!"

"Do you notice how almighty quiet everything's gone the last half-hour or so?" I said a little later. "It must be the mist thickening down."

"It is the mist," said the mate, going to the rail and staring out. "Good Lord, what's that?" he added.

Something had knocked his hat from his head, and it fell with a sharp rap at my feet. And suddenly, you know, I got a premonition of something horrid.

"Come away from the rail, sir!" I said sharply, and gave one jump and caught him by the shoulders and dragged him back. "Come away from the side!"

"What's up, mister?" he growled at me, an twisted his shoulders free. "What's wrong with you? Was it you knocked off my cap?" He stooped and felt around for it, and as he did so I *heard* something unmistakably fiddling away at the rail which the mate had just left.

"My God, sir!" I said "there's something there. Hark!"

The mate stiffened up, listening; then he heard it. It was for all the world as if something was feeling and rubbing the rail there in the darkness, not two fathoms away from us.

"Who's there?" said the mate quickly. Then, as there was no answer: "What the devil's this hanky-panky? Who's playing the goat there?" He made a swift step through the darkness towards he rail, but I caught him by the elbow.

"Don't go, mister!" I said, hardly above a whisper. "It's not one of the men. Let me get a light."

"Quick, then!" he said, and I turned and ran aft to the binnacle and snatched out the lighted lamp. As I did so I heard the mate shout something out of the darkness in a strange voice. There came a sharp, loud, rattling sound, and then a crash, and immediately the mate roaring to me to hasten with the light. His voice changed even whilst he shouted, and gave out somthing that was nearer a scream than anything else. There came two loud, dull blows and an extraordinary gasping sound; and then, as I raced along the poop, there was a tremendous smashing of glass and an immediate silence.

"Mr. Lammart!" I shouted. "Mr. Lammart!" And then I had reached the place where I had left the mate for forty seconds before; but he was not there.

"Mr. Lammart!" I shouted again, holding the light high over my head and turning quickly to look behind me. As I did so my foot glided on some slippery substance, and I went headlong to the deck with a tremendous thud, smashing the lamp and putting out the light.

I was on my feet again in an instant. I groped a moment for the lamp, and as I did so I heard the men singing out from the maindeck and the noise of their feet as they came running aft. I found the broken lamp and realised it was useless; then I jumped for the companion-way, and in half a minute I was back with the big saloon lamp glaring bright in my hands.

I ran for'ard again, shielding the upper edge of the glass chimney from the draught of my running, and the blaze of the big lamp seemed to make the weather side of the poop as bright as day, except for the mist, that gave something of a vagueness to things.

Where I had left the mate there was blood upon the deck, but nowhere any signs of the man himself. I ran to the weather rail and held the lamp to it. There was blood upon it, and the rail itself seemed to have been wrenched by some huge force. I put out my hand and found that I could shake it. Then I leaned out-board and held the lamp at arm's length, staring down over the ship's side.

"Mr. Lammart!" I shouted into the night and the thick mist. "Mr. Lammart! Mr. Lammart!" But my voice seemed to go, lost and muffled and infinitely small, away into the billowy darkness.

I heard the men snuffling and breathing, waiting to leeward of the poop. I whirled round to them, holding the lamp high,

"We heard somethin', sir," said Tarpley, the leading seaman in our watch. "Is anythin' wrong, sir?"

"The mate's gone," I said blankly. "We heard something, and I went for the binnacle lamp. Then he shouted, and I heard a sound of things smashing, and when I got back he'd gone clean." I turned and held the light out again over the unseen sea, and the men crowded round along the rail and stared, bewildered.

"Blood, sir," said Tarpley, pointing. "There's somethin' almighty queer out there." He waved a huge hand into the darkness. "That's what stinks —"

He never finished; for suddenly one of the men cried out something in a frightened voice: "Look out, sir! Look out, sir!"

I saw, in one brief flash of sight, something come in with an infernal flicker of movement; and then, before I could form any notion of what I had seen, the lamp was dashed to pieces across the poop deck. In that instant my perceptions cleared, and I saw the incredible folly of what we were doing; for there we were, standing up against the blank, un-knowable night, and out there in the darkness there surely lurked some thing of monstrousness; and we were at its mercy. I seemed to feel it hovering — hovering over us, so that I felt the sickening creep of goose-flesh all over me.

"Stand back from the rail!" I shouted. "Stand back from the rail!" There was a rush of feet as the men obeyed, in sudden apprehension of their danger, and I gave back with them. Even as I did so I felt some invisible thing brush my shoulder, and an indescribable smell was in my nostrils from something that moved over me in the dark.

"Down into the saloon everyone!" I shouted. "Down with you all! Don't wait a moment!"

There was a rush along the dark weather deck, and then the men went helter-skelter down the companion steps into the saloon, falling and cursing over one another in the darkness. I sang out to the man at the wheel to join them, and then I followed.

I came upon the men huddled at the foot of the stairs and filling up the passage, all crowding each other in the darkness. The skipper's voice was filling the saloon, and he was demanding in violent adjectives the cause of so tremendous a noise. From the steward's berth there came also a voice and the splutter of a match, and then the glow of a lamp in the saloon itself.

I pushed my way through the men and found the captain in the saloon in his sleeping gear, looking both drowsy and angry, though perhaps bewilderment topped every other feeling. He held his cabin lamp in his hand, and shone the light over the huddle of men.

I hurried to explain, and told him of the incredible disappearance of the mate, and of my conviction that some extraordinary thing was lurking near the ship out in the mist and the darkness. I mentioned the curious smell, and told how the mate had suggested that we had drifted down near some old-time, sea-rotted derelict. And, you know, even as I put it into awkward words, my imagination began to awaken to horrible discomforts; a thousand dreadful impossibilities of the sea became suddenly possible.

The captain (Jeldy was his name) did not stop to dress, but ran back into his cabin, and came out in a few moments with a couple of revolvers and a handful of cartridges. The second mate had come running out of his cabin at the noise, and had listed intensely to what I had to say; and now he jumped back into his berth and brought out his own lamp and a large Smith and Wesson, which was evidently ready loaded.

Captain Jeldy pushed one of his revolvers into my hands, with some of the cartridges, and we began hastily to load the weapons. Then the captain caught up his lamp and made for the stairway, ordering the men into the saloon out of his way.

"Shall you want them, sir?" I asked.

"No," he said. "It's no use their running any unnecessary risks." He threw a word over his shoulder: "Stay quiet here, men; if I want you I'll give you a shout; then come spry!"

"Aye, aye, sir," said the watch in a chorus; and then I was following the captain up the stairs, with the second mate close behind.

We came up through the companion-way on to the silence of the deserted poop. The mist had thickened up, even during the brief time that I had been below, and there was not a breath of wind. The mist was so dense that it seemed to press in upon us, and the two lamps made a kind of luminous halo in the mist, which seemed to absorb their light in a most peculiar way.

"Where was he?" the captain asked me, almost in a whisper.

"On the port side, sir," I said, "a little foreside the charthouse and about a dozen feet in from the rail. I'll show you the exact place."

We went for'ard along what had been the weather side, going quietly and watchfully, though, indeed, it was little enough that we could see, because of the mist. Once, as I led the way, I thought I heard a vague sound somewhere in the mist, but was all unsure because of the slow creak, creak of the spars and gear as the vessel rolled slightly upon an odd, oily swell. Apart from this slight sound, and the far-up rustle of the canvas slatting gently against the masts, there was no sound of all throughout the ship. I assure you the silence seemed to me to be almost menacing, in the tense, nervous state in which I was.

"Hereabouts is where I left him," I whispered to the captain a few seconds later. "Hold your lamp low, sir. There's blood on the deck."

Captain Jeldy did so, and made a slight sound with his mouth at what he saw. Then, heedless of my hurried warning, he walked across to the rail, holding his lamp high up. I followed him, for I could not let him go alone; and the second mate came too, with his lamp. They leaned over the port rail and held their lamps out into the mist and the unknown darkness beyond the ship's side. I remember how the lamps made just two yellow glares in the mist, ineffectual, yet serving somehow to make extraordinarily plain the vastitude of the night and the *possibilities of the dark*. Perhaps that is a queer way to put it, but it gives you the effect of that moment upon my feelings. And all the time, you know, there was upon me the brutal, frightening expectancy of something reaching in at us from out of that everlasting darkness and mist that held all the sea and the night, so that we were just three mist-shrouded, hidden figures, peering nervously.

The mist was now so thick that we could not even see the surface of the water overside, and fore and aft of us the rail vanished away into the fog and the dark. And then, as we stood here staring, I heard something moving down on the maindeck. I caught Captain Jeldy by the elbow.

"Come away from the rail, sir," I said, hardly above a whisper; and he, with the swift premonition of danger, stepped back and allowed me to urge him well inboard. The second mate followed, and the three of us stood there in the mist, staring round about us and holding our revolvers handily, and the dull waves of the mist beating in slowly upon the lamps in vague wreathings and swirls of fog.

"What was it you heard, mister?" asked the captain after a few moments.

"Ssst!" I muttered. "There it is again. There's something moving down on the maindeck!"

Captain Jeldy heard it himself now, and the three of us stood listening intensely. Yet it was hard to know what to make of the sounds. And then suddenly there was the rattle of a deck ringbolt, and then again, as if something or someone were fumbling and playing with it.

"Down there on the maindeck!" shouted the captain abruptly, his voice seeming hoarse close to my ear, yet immediately smothered by the fog. "Down there on the maindeck! Who's there?"

But there came never an answering sound. And the three of us stood there, looking quickly this way and that, and listening. Abruptly the second mate muttered something:

"The look-out, sir! The look-out!"

Captain Jeldy took the hint on the instant.

"On the look-out there!" he shouted.

And then, far away and muffled-sounding, there came the answering cry of the look-out man from the fo'c'sle head:

"Sir-r-r?" A little voice, long drawn out through unknowable alleys of fog.

"Go below into the fo'c'sle and shut both doors, an' don't stir out till you're told!" sung out Captain Jeldy, his voice going lost into the mist. And then the man's answering "Aye, aye, sir!" coming to us faint and mournful. And directly afterwards the clang of a steel door, hollow-sounding and remote; and immediately the sound of another.

"That puts them safe for the present, anyway," said the second mate. And even as he spoke there came again that indefinite noise down upon the maindeck of something moving with an incredible and unnatural stealthiness.

"On the maindeck there!" shouted Captain Jeldy sternly. "If there is anyone there, answer, or I shall fire!"

The reply was both amazing and terrifying, for suddenly a tremendous blow was stricken upon the deck, and then there came the dull, rolling sound of some enormous weight going hollowly across the maindeck. And then an abominable silence.

"My God!' said Captain Jeldy in a low voice, "what was *that?*" And he raised his pistol, but I caught him by the wrist. "Don't shoot, sir!" I whispered. "It'll be no good. That — that — whatever it is I — mean it's something enormous, sir. I — I really wouldn't shoot ." I found it impossible to put my vague idea into words; but I felt there was a force aboard, down on the maindeck, that it would be futile to attack with so ineffectual a thing as a puny revolver bullet.

And then, as I held Captain Jeldy's wrist, and he hesitated, irresolute, there came a sudden bleating of sheep and the sound of lashings being burst and the cracking of wood; and the next instant a huge crash, followed by crash after crash, and the anguished m-aa-a-a-ing of sheep.

"My God!" said the second mate, "the sheep-pen's being beaten to pieces against the deck. Good God! What sort of thing could do that?"

The tremendous beating ceased, and there was a splashing overside; and after that a silence so profound that it seemed as if the whole atmosphere of the night was full of an unbearable, tense quietness. And then the damp slatting of a sail, far up in the night, that made me start — a lonesome sound to break suddenly through that infernal silence upon my raw nerves.

"Get below, both of you. Smartly now!" muttered Captain Jeldy. "There's something run either aboard us or alongside; and we can't do anything till daylight."

We went below and shut the doors of the companion-way, and there we lay in the wide Atlantic, without wheel or look-out or officer in charge, and something incredible down on the dark maindeck.

## II.

FOR some hours we sat in the captain's cabin talking the matter over whilst the watch slept, sprawled in a dozen attitudes on the floor of the saloon. Captain Jeldy and the second mate still wore their pyjamas, and our loaded revolvers lay handy on the cabin table. And so we watched anxiously through the hours for the dawn to come in.

As the light strengthened we endeavoured to get some view of the sea from the ports, but the mist was so thick about us that it was exactly like looking out into a grey nothingness, that became presently white as the day came.

"Now," said Captain Jeldy, "we're going to look into this."

He went out through the saloon to the companion stairs. At the top he opened the two doors, and the mist rolled in on us, white and impenetrable. For a little while we stood there, the three of us, absolutely silent and listening, with our revolvers handy; but never a sound came to us except the odd, vague slatting of a sail or the slight creaking of the gear as the ship lifted on some slow, invisible swell.

Presently the captain stepped cautiously out on to the deck; he was in his cabin slippers, and therefore made no sound. I was wearing gum-boots, and followed him silently, and the second mate after me in his bare feet. Captain Jeldy went a few paces along the deck, and the mist hid him utterly. "Phew!" I heard him mutter, "the stink's worse than ever!" His voice came odd and vague to me through the wreathing of the mist.

"The sun'll soon eat up all this fog," said the second mate at my elbow, in a voice little above a whisper.

We stepped after the captain, and found him a couple of fathoms away, standing shrouded in the mist in an attitude of tense listening.

"Can't hear a thing!" he whispered. "We'll go for'ard to the break, as quiet as you like. Don't make a sound."

We went forward, like three shadows, and suddenly Captain Jeldy kicked his shin against something and pitched headlong over it, making a tremendous noise. He got up quickly, swearing grimly, and the three of us stood there in silence, waiting lest any infernal thing should come upon us out of all that white invisibility. Once I felt sure I saw something coming towards me, and I raised my revolver, but saw in a moment that there was nothing. The tension of imminent, nervous expectancy eased from us, and Captain Jeldy stooped over the object on the deck.

"The port hencoop's been shifted out here!" he muttered. "It's all stove!"

"That must be what I heard last night when the mate went," I whispered. There was a loud crash just before he sang out to me to hurry with the lamp."

Captain Jeldy left the smashed hencoop, and the three of us tiptoed silently to the rail across the break of the poop. Here we leaned over and stared down into the blank whiteness of the mist that hid everything.

"Can't see a thing," whispered the second mate; yet as he spoke I could fancy that I heard a slight, indefinite, slurring noise somewhere below us; and I caught them each by an arm to draw them back.

"There's something down there," I muttered. "For goodness' sake come back from the rail."

We gave back a step or two, and then stopped to listen; and even as we did so there came a slight air playing through the mist.

"The breeze is coming," said the second mate. "Look, the mist is clearing already."

He was right. Already the look of white impenetrability had gone, and suddenly we could see the corner of the after-hatch coamings through the thinning fog. Within a minute we could see as far for'ard as the mainmast, and then the stuff blew away from us, clear of the vessel, like a great wall of whiteness, that dissipated as it went.

"*Look!*" we all exclaimed together. The whole of the vessel was now clear to our sight; but it was not at the ship herself that we looked, for, after one quick glance along the empty maindeck, we had seen something beyond the ship's side. All around the vessel there lay a submerged spread of weed, for, maybe, a good quarter of a mile upon every side.

"Weed!" sang out Captain Jeldy in a voice of comprehension. "Weed!

Look! By Jove, I guess I know now what got the mate!"

He turned and ran to the port side and looked over. And suddenly he stiffened and beckoned silently over his shoulder to us to come and see. We had followed, and now we stood, one on each side of him, staring.

"Look!" whispered the captain, pointing. "See the great brute! Do you see it? There! Look!"

At first I could see nothing except the submerged spread of the weed, into which we had evidently run after dark. Then, as I stared intently, my gaze began to separate from the surrounding weed a leathery-looking something that was somewhat darker in hue than the weed itself.

"My God!" said Captain Jeldy. "What a monster! What a monster! Just look at the brute! Look at the thing's eyes! That's what got the mate. What a creature out of hell itself!"

I saw it plainly now; three of the massive feelers lay twined in and out among the clumpings of the weed; and then, abruptly, I realised that the two extraordinary round disks, motionless and inscrutable, were the creature's eyes, just below the surface of the water. It appeared to be staring, expressionless, up at the steel side of the vessel. I traced, vaguely, the shapeless monstrosity of what must be termed its head. "My God!" I muttered. "It's an enormous squid of some kind! What an awful brute! What —"

The sharp report of the captain's revolver came at that moment. He had fired at the thing, and instantly there was a most awful commotion alongside. The weed was hove upward, literally in tons. An enormous quantity was thrown aboard us by the thrashing of the monster's great feelers. The sea seemed almost to boil, in one great cauldron of weed and water, all about the brute, and the steel side of the ship resounded with the dull, tremendous blows that the creature gave in its struggle. And into all that whirling boil of tentacles, weed, and seawater the three of us emptied our revolvers as fast as we could fire and reload. I remember the feeling of fierce satisfaction I had in thus aiding to avenge the death of the mate.

Suddenly the captain roared out to us to jump back, and we obeyed on the instant. As we did so the weed rose up into a great mound over twenty feet in height, and more than a ton of it slopped aboard. The next instant three of the monstrous tentacles came in over the side, and the vessel gave a slow, sullen roll to port as the weight came upon her, for the monster had literally hove itself almost free of the sea against our port side, in one vast, leathery shape, all wreathed with weed-fronds, and seeming drenched with blood and curious black liquid.

The feelers that had come inboard thrashed round here and there, and suddenly one of them curled in the most hideous, snake-like fashion around the base of the mainmast. This seemed to attract it, for immediately it curled the two others about the mast, and forthwith wrenched upon it with such hideous violence that the whole towering length of spars, through all their height of a hundred and fifty feet, were shaken visibly, whilst the vessel herself vibrated with the stupendous efforts of the brute.

"It'll have the mast down, sir!" said the second mate, with a gasp. "My God! It'll strain her side open! My —"

"One of those blasting cartridges!" I said to Jeldy almost in a shout, as the inspiration took me. "Blow the brute to pieces!"

"Get one, quick!" said the captain, jerking his thumb towards the companion. "You know where they are."

In thirty seconds I was back with the cartridge. Captain Jeldy took out his knife and cut the fuse dead short; then, with a steady hand, he lit the fuse, and calmly held it, until I backed away, shouting to him to throw it, for I knew it must explode in another couple of seconds.

Captain Jeldy threw the thing like one throws a quoit, so that it fell into the sea just on the outward side of the vast bulk of the monster. So well had he timed it that it burst, with a stunning report, just as it struck the water. The effect upon the squid was amazing. It seemed literally to collapse. The enormous tentacles released themselves from the mast and curled across the deck helplessly, and were drawn inertly over the rail, as the enormous bulk sank away from the ship's side, out of sight, into the weed. The ship rolled slowly to starboard, and then steadied. "Thank God!" I muttered, and looked at the two others. They were pallid and sweating, and I must have been the same.

"Here's the breeze again," said the second mate, a minute later. "We're moving." He turned, without another word, and raced aft to the wheel, whilst the vessel slid over and through the weedfield.

"Look where that brute broke up the sheep-pen!" cried Jeldy, pointing. "And here's the skylight of the sail-locker smashed to bits!"

He walked across to it, and glanced down. And suddenly he let out a tremendous shout of astonishment:

"Here's the mate down here!" he shouted. "He's not overboard at all! He's *here!*"

He dropped himself down through the skylight on to the sails, and I after him; and, surely, there was the mate, lying all huddled and insensible on a hummock of spare sails. In his right hand he held a drawn sheath-knife, which he was in the habit of carrying A. B. fashion, whilst his left hand was all caked with dried blood, where he had been badly cut. Afterwards, we concluded he had cut himself in slashing at one of the tentacles of the squid, which had caught him round the left wrist, the tip of the tentacle being still curled tight about his arm, just as it had been when he hacked it through. For the rest, he was not seriously damaged, the creature having obviously flung him violently away through the framework of the skylight, so that he had fallen in a studded condition on to the pile of sails.

We got him on deck, and down into his bunk, where we left the steward to attend to him. When we returned to the poop the vessel had drawn clear of the weed-field, and the captain and I stopped for a few moments to stare astern over the taffrail.

As we stood and looked something wavered up out of the heart of the weed — a long, tapering, sinous thing, that curled and wavered against the dawn-light, and presently sank back again into the demure weed — a veritable spider of the deep, waiting in the great web that Dame Nature had spun for it in the eddy of her tides and currents.

And we sailed away northwards, with strengthening "trades," and left that patch of monstrousness to the loneliness of the sea.

# THE VOICE IN THE NIGHT

IT WAS a dark, starless night. We were becalmed in the Northern Pacific. Our exact position I do not know; for the sun had been hidden during the course of a weary, breathless week, by a thin haze which had seemed to float above us, about the height of our mastheads, at whiles descending and shrouding the surrounding sea.

With there being no wind, we had steadied the tiller, and I was the only man on deck. The crew, consisting of two men and a boy, were sleeping forrard in their den; while Will — my friend, and the master of our little craft — was aft in his bunk on the port side of the little cabin.

Suddenly, from out of the surrounding darkness, there came a hail: "Schooner, ahoy!"

The cry was so unexpected that I gave no immediate answer, because of my surprise.

It came again — a voice curiously throaty and inhuman, calling from somewhere upon the dark sea away on our port broadside:

"Schooner, ahoy!"

"Hullo!" I sung out, having gathered my wits somewhat. "What are you? What do you want?"

"You need not be afraid," answered the queer voice, having probably noticed some trace of confusion in my tone. "I am only an old man."

The pause sounded oddly; but it was only afterwards that it came back to me with any significance.

"Why don't you come alongside, then?" I queried somewhat snappishly; for I liked not his hinting at my having been a trifle shaken.

"I — I — can't. It wouldn't be safe. I —" The voice broke off, and there was silence.

"What do you mean?" I asked, growing more and more astonished. "Why not safe? Where are you?"

I listened for a moment; but there came no answer. And then, a sudden indefinite suspicion, of I knew not what, coming to me, I stepped swiftly to the binnacle, and took out the lighted lamp. At the same time, I knocked on the deck with my heel to waken Will. Then I was back at the side, throwing the yellow funnel of light out into the silent immensity beyond our rail. As I did so, I heard a slight, muffled cry, and then the sound of a splash as though someone had dipped oars abruptly. Yet I cannot say that I saw anything with certainty; save, it seemed to me, that with the first flash of the light, there had been something upon the waters, where now there was nothing.

"Hullo, there!" I called. "What foolery is this!"

But there came only the indistinct sounds of a boat being pulled away into the night.

Then I heard Will's voice, from the direction of the after scuttle:

"What's up, George?"

"Come here, Will!" I said.

"What is it?" he asked, coming across the deck.

I told him the queer thing which had happened. He put several questions; then, after a moment's silence, he raised his hands to his lips, and hailed:

"Boat, ahoy!"

From a long distance away there came back to us a faint reply, and my companion repeated his call. Presently, after a short period of silence, there grew on our hearing the muffled sound of oars; at which Will hailed again.

This time there was a reply:

"Put away the light."

"I'm damned if I will," I muttered; but Will told me to do as the voice bade, and I shoved it down under the bulwarks.

"Come nearer," he said, and the oar-strokes continued. Then, when apparently some half-dozen fathoms distant, they again ceased.

"Come alongside," exclaimed Will. "There's nothing to be frightened of aboard here!"

"Promise that you will not show the light?"

"What's to do with you," I burst out, "that you're so infernally afraid of the light?"

"Because —" began the voice, and stopped short.

"Because what?" I asked quickly.

Will put his hand on my shoulder.

"Shut up a minute, old man," he said, in a low voice. "Let me tackle him."

He leant more over the rail.

"See here, Mister," he said, "this is a pretty queer business, you coming upon us like this, right out in the middle of the blessed Pacific. How are we to know what sort of a hanky-panky trick you're up to? You say there's only one of you. How are we to know, unless we get a squint at you — eh? What's your objection to the light, anyway?"

As he finished, I heard the noise of the oars again, and then the voice came; but now from a greater distance, and sounding extremely hopeless and pathetic.

"I am sorry — sorry! I would not have troubled you, only I am hungry, and — so is she."

The voice died away, and the sound of the oars, dipping irregularly, was borne to us.

"Stop!" sung out Will. "I don't want to drive you away. Come back! We'll keep the light hidden, if you don't like it."

He turned to me:

"It's a damned queer rig, this; but I think there's nothing to be afraid of?"

There was a question in his tone, and I replied.

"No, I think the poor devil's been wrecked around here, and gone crazy."

The sound of the oars drew nearer.

"Shove that lamp back in the binnacle," said Will; then he leaned over the rail and listened. I replaced the lamp, and came back to his side. The dipping of the oars ceased some dozen yards distant.

"Won't you come alongside now?" asked Will in an even voice. "I have had the lamp put back in the binnacle."

"I — I cannot," replied the voice. "I dare not come nearer. I dare not even pay you for the — the provisions."

"That's all right," said Will, and hesitated. "You're welcome to as much grub as you can take —" Again he hesitated.

"You are very good," exclaimed the voice. "May God, Who understands everything, reward you —" It broke off huskily.

"The — the lady?" said Will abruptly. "Is she —"

"I have left her behind upon the island," came the voice.

"What island?" I cut in.

"I know not its name," returned the voice. "I would to God —!" it began, and checked itself as suddenly.

"Could we not send a boat for her?" asked Will at this point.

"No!" said the voice, with extraordinary emphasis. "My God! No!" There was a moment's pause; then it added, in a tone which seemed a merited reproach:

"It was because of our want I ventured — because her agony tortured me."

"I am a forgetful brute," exclaimed Will. "Just wait a minute, whoever you are, and I will bring you up something at once."

In a couple of minutes he was back again, and his arms were full of various edibles. He paused at the rail.

"Can't you come alongside for them?" he asked.

"No — I *dare not*," replied the voice, and it seemed to me that in its tones I detected a note of stifled craving — as though the owner hushed a mortal desire. It came to me then in a flash, that the poor old creature out there in the darkness, was *suffering* for actual need of that which Will held in his arms; and yet, because of some unintelligible dread, refraining from dashing to the side of our little schooner, and receiving it. And with the lightning-like conviction, there came the knowledge that the Invisible was not mad; but sanely facing some intolerable horror.

"Damn it, Will!" I said, full of many feelings, over which predominated a vast sympathy. "Get a box. We must float off the stuff to him in it."

This we did — propelling it away from the vessel, out into the darkness, by means of a boathook. In a minute, a slight cry from the Invisible came to us, and we knew that he had secured the box.

A little later, he called out a farewell to us, and so heartful a blessing, that I am sure we were the better for it. Then, without more ado, we heard the ply of oars across the darkness.

"Pretty soon off," remarked Will, with perhaps just a little sense of injury.

"Wait," I replied. "I think somehow he'll come back. He must have been badly needing that food."

"And the lady," said Will. For a moment he was silent; then he continued:

"It's the queerest thing ever I've tumbled across, since I've been fishing."

"Yes," I said, and fell to pondering.

And so the time slipped away — an hour, another, and still Will stayed with me; for the queer adventure had knocked all desire for sleep out of him.

The third hour was three parts through, when we heard again the sound of oars across the silent ocean.

"Listen!" said Will, a low note of excitement in his voice.

"He's coming, just as I thought," I muttered.

The dipping of the oars grew nearer, and I noted that the strokes were firmer and longer. The food had been needed.

They came to a stop a little distance off the broadside, and the queer voice came again to us through the darkness:

"Schooner, ahoy!"

"That you?" asked Will.

"Yes," replied the voice. "I left you suddenly; but — but there was great need."

"The lady?" questioned Will.

"The — lady is grateful now on earth. She will be more grateful soon in — in heaven."

Will began to make some reply, in a puzzled voice; but became confused, and broke off short. I said nothing. I was wondering at the curious pauses, and, apart from my wonder, I was full of a great sympathy.

The voice continued:

"We — she and I, have talked, as we shared the result of God's tenderness and yours —"

Will interposed; but without coherence.

"I beg of you not to — to belittle your deed of Christian charity this night," said the voice. "Be sure that it has not escaped His notice."

It stopped, and there was a full minute's silence. Then it came again:

"We have spoken together upon that which — which has befallen us. We had thought to go out, without telling any, of the terror which has come into our — lives. She is with me in believing that to-night's happenings are under a special ruling, and that it is God's wish that we should tell to you all that we have suffered since — since —"

"Yes?" said Will softly.

"Since the sinking of the Albatross."

"Ah!" I exclaimed involuntarily. "She left Newcastle for 'Frisco some six months ago, and hasn't been heard of since."

"Yes," answered the voice. "But some few degrees to the North of the line she was caught in a terrible storm, and dismasted. When the day came, it was found that she was leaking badly, and, presently, it falling to a calm, the sailors took to the boats, leaving — leaving a young lady — my fiancée — and myself upon the wreck.

"We were below, gathering together a few of our belongings, when they left. They were entirely callous, through fear, and when we came up upon the deck, we saw them only as small shapes afar off upon the horizon. Yet we did not despair, but set to work and constructed a small raft. Upon this we put such few matters as it would hold including a quantity of water and some ship's biscuit. Then, the vessel being very deep in the water, we got ourselves on to the raft, and pushed off.

"It was later, when I observed that we seemed to be in the way of some tide or current, which bore us from the ship at an angle; so that in the course of three hours, by my watch, her hull became invisible to our sight, her broken masts remaining in view for a somewhat longer period. Then, towards evening, it grew misty, and so through the night. The next day we were still encompassed by the mist, the weather remaining quiet.

"For four days we drifted through this strange haze, until, on the evening of the fourth day, there grew upon our ears the murmur of breakers at a distance. Gradually it became plainer, and, somewhat after midnight, it appeared to sound upon either hand at no very great space. The raft was raised upon a swell several times, and then we were in smooth water, and the noise of the breakers was behind.

"When the morning came, we found that we were in a sort of great lagoon; but of this we noticed little at the time; for close before us, through the enshrouding mist, loomed the hull of a large sailing-vessel. With one accord, we fell upon our knees and thanked God; for we thought that here was an end to our perils. We had much to learn.

"The raft drew near to the ship, and we shouted on them to take us aboard; but none answered. Presently the raft touched against the side of the vessel, and, seeing a rope hanging downwards, I seized it and began to climb. Yet I had much ado to make my way up, because of a kind of grey, lichenous fungus which had seized upon the rope, and which blotched the side of the ship lividly.

"I reached the rail and clambered over it, on to the deck. Here I saw that the decks were covered, in great patches, with grey masses, some of them rising into nodules several feet in height; but at the time I thought less of this matter than of the possibility of there being people aboard the ship. I shouted; but none answered. Then I went to the door below the poop deck. I opened it, and peered in. There was a great smell of staleness, so that I knew in a moment that nothing living was within, and with the knowledge, I shut the door quickly; for I felt suddenly lonely.

"I went back to the side where I had scrambled up. My — my sweetheart was still sitting quietly upon the raft. Seeing me look down she called up to know whether there were any aboard of the ship. I replied that the vessel had the appearance of having been long deserted; but that if she would wait a little I would see whether there was anything in the shape of a ladder by which she could ascend to the deck. Then we would make a search through the vessel together. A little later, on the opposite side of the decks, I found a rope side-ladder. This I carried across, and a minute afterwards she was beside me.

"Together we explored the cabins and apartments in the after part of the ship; but nowhere was there any sign of life. Here and there within the cabins themselves, we came across odd patches of that queer fungus; but this, as my sweetheart said, could be cleansed away.

"In the end, having assured ourselves that the after portion of the vessel was empty, we picked our ways to the bows, between the ugly grey nodules of that strange growth; and here we made a further search which told us that there was indeed none aboard but ourselves.

"This being now beyond any doubt, we returned to the stern of the ship and proceeded to make ourselves as comfortable as possible. Together we cleared out and cleaned two of the cabins: and after that I made examination whether there was anything eatable in the ship. This I soon found was so, and thanked God in my heart for His goodness. In addition to this I discovered the whereabouts of the fresh-water pump, and having fixed it I found the water drinkable, though somewhat unpleasant to the taste.

"For several days we stayed aboard the ship, without attempting to get to the shore. We were busily engaged in making the place habitable. Yet even thus early we became aware that our lot was even less to be desired than might have been imagined; for though, as a first step, we scraped away the odd patches of growth that studded the floors and walls of the cabins and saloon, yet they returned almost to their original size within the space of twenty-four hours, which not only discouraged us, but gave us a feeling of vague unease.

"Still we would not admit ourselves beaten, so set to work afresh, and not only scraped away the fungus, but soaked the places where it had been, with carbolic, a can-full of which I had found in the pantry. Yet, by the end of the week the growth had returned in full strength, and, in addition, it had spread to other places, as though our touching it had allowed germs from it to travel elsewhere.

"On the seventh morning, my sweetheart woke to find a small patch of it growing on her pillow, close to her face. At that, she came to me, so soon as she could get her garments upon her. I was in the galley at the time lighting the fire for breakfast.

"Come here, John," she said, and led me aft. When I saw the thing upon her pillow I shuddered, and then and there we agreed to go right out of the ship and see whether we could not fare to make ourselves more comfortable ashore.

"Hurriedly we gathered together our few belongings, and even among these I found that the fungus had been at work; for one of her shawls had a little lump of it growing near one edge. I threw the whole thing over the side, without saying anything to her.

"The raft was still alongside, but it was too clumsy to guide, and I lowered down a small boat that hung across the stern, and in this we made our way to the shore. Yet, as we drew near to it, I became gradually aware that here the vile fungus, which had driven us from the ship, was growing riot. In places it rose into horrible, fantastic mounds, which seemed almost to quiver, as with a quiet life, when the wind blew across them. Here and there it took on the forms of vast fingers, and in others it just spread out flat and smooth and treacherous. Odd places, it appeared as grotesque stunted trees, seeming extraordinarily kinked and gnarled — the whole quaking vilely at times.

"At first, it seemed to us that there was no single portion of the surrounding shore which was not hidden beneath the masses of the hideous lichen; yet, in this, I found we were mistaken; for somewhat later, coasting along the shore at a little distance, we descried a smooth white patch of what appeared to be fine sand, and there we landed. It was not sand. What it was I do not know. All that I have observed is that upon it the fungus will not grow; while everywhere else, save where the sand-like earth wanders oddly, path-wise, amid the grey desolation of the lichen, there is nothing but that loathsome greyness.

"It is difficult to make you understand how cheered we were to find one place that was absolutely free from the growth, and here we deposited our belongings. Then we went back to the ship for such things as it seemed to us we should need. Among other matters, I managed to bring ashore with me one of the ship's sails, with which I constructed two small tents, which, though exceedingly rough-shaped, served the purpose for which they were intended. In these we lived and stored our various necessities, and thus for a matter of some four weeks all went smoothly and without particular unhappiness. Indeed, I may say with much of happiness — for — for we were together.

"It was on the thumb of her right hand that the growth first showed. It was only a small circular spot, much like a little grey mole. My God! how the fear leapt to my heart when she showed me the place. We cleansed it, between us, washing it with carbolic and water. In the morning of the following day she showed her hand to me again. The grey warty thing had returned. For a little while, we looked at one another in silence. Then, still wordless, we started again to remove it. In the midst of the operation she spoke suddenly.

" 'What's that on the side of your face, dear?' Her voice was sharp with anxiety. I put my hand up to feel.

" 'There! Under the hair by your ear. A little to the front a bit.' My finger rested upon the place, and then I knew.

" 'Let us get your thumb done first,' I said. And she submitted, only because she was afraid to touch me until it was cleansed. I finished washing and disinfecting her thumb, and then she turned to my face. After it was finished we sat together and talked awhile of many things for there had come into our lives sudden, very terrible thoughts. We were, all at once, afraid of something worse than death. We spoke of loading the boat with provisions and water and making our way out on to the sea; yet we were helpless, for many causes, and — and the growth had attacked us already. We decided to stay. God would do with us what was His will. We would wait.

"A month, two months, three months passed and the places grew somewhat, and there had come others. Yet we fought so strenuously with the fear that its headway was but slow, comparatively speaking.

"Occasionally we ventured off to the ship for such stores as we needed. There we found that the fungus grew persistently. One of the nodules on the maindeck became soon as high as my head.

"We had now given up all thought or hope of leaving the island. We had realized that it would be unallowable to go among healthy humans, with the things from which we were suffering.

"With this determination and knowledge in our minds we knew that we should have to husband our food and water; for we did not know, at that time, but that we should possibly live for many years.

"This reminds me that I have told you that I am an old man. Judged by the years this is not so. But — but —"

He broke off; then continued somewhat abruptly:

"As I was saying, we knew that we should have to use care in the matter of food. But we had no idea then how little food there was left of which to take care. It was a week later that I made the discovery that all the other bread tanks — which I had supposed full — were empty, and that (beyond odd tins of vegetables and meat, and some other matters) we had nothing on which to depend, but the bread in the tank which I had already opened.

"After learning this I bestirred myself to do what I could, and set to work at fishing in the lagoon; but with no success. At this I was somewhat inclined to feel desperate until the thought came to me to try outside the lagoon, in the open sea.

"Here, at times, I caught odd fish; but so infrequently that they proved of but little help in keeping us from the hunger which threatened.

It seemed to me that our deaths were likely to come by hunger, and not by the growth of the thing which had seized upon our bodies.

"We were in this state of mind when the fourth month wore out. When I made a very horrible discovery. One morning, a little before midday. I came off from the ship with a portion of the biscuits which were left. In the mouth of her tent I saw my sweetheart sitting, eating something.

" 'What is it, my dear?' I called out as I leapt ashore. Yet, on hearing my voice, she seemed confused, and, turning, slyly threw something towards the edge of the little clearing. It fell short, and a vague suspicion having arisen within me, I walked across and picked it up. It was a piece of the grey fungus.

"As I went to her with it in my hand, she turned deadly pale; then rose red.

"I felt strangely dazed and frightened.

" 'My dear! My dear!' I said, and could say no more. Yet at words she broke down and cried bitterly. Gradually, as she calmed, I got from her the news that she had tried it the preceding day, and — and liked it. I got her to promise on her knees not to touch it again, however great our hunger. After she had promised she told me that the desire for it had come suddenly, and that, until the moment of desire, she had experienced nothing towards it but the most extreme repulsion.

"Later in the day, feeling strangely restless, and much shaken with the thing which I had discovered, I made my way along one of the twisted paths — formed by the white, sand-like substance — which led among the fungoid growth. I had, once before, ventured along there; but not to any great distance. This time, being involved in perplexing thought, I went much further than hitherto.

"Suddenly I was called to myself by a queer hoarse sound on my left. Turning quickly I saw that there was movement among an extraordinarily shaped mass of fungus, close to my elbow. It was swaying uneasily, as though it possessed life of its own. Abruptly, as I stared, the thought came to me that the thing had a grotesque resemblance to the figure of a distorted human creature. Even as the fancy flashed into my brain, there was a slight, sickening noise of tearing, and I saw that one of the branch-like arms was detaching itself from the surrounding grey masses, and coming towards me. The head of the thing — a shapeless grey ball, inclined in my direction. I stood stupidly, and the vile arm brushed across my face. I gave out a frightened cry, and ran back a few paces. There was a sweetish taste upon my lips where the thing had touched me. I licked them, and was immediately filled with an inhuman desire. I turned and seized a mass of the fungus. Then more and — more. I was insatiable. In the midst of devouring, the remembrance of the morning's discovery swept into my mazed brain. It was sent by God. I dashed the fragment I held to the ground. Then, utterly wretched and feeling a dreadful guiltiness, I made my way back to the little encampment.

"I think she knew, by some marvellous intuition which love must have given, so soon as she set eyes on me. Her quiet sympathy made it easier for me, and I told her of my sudden weakness; yet omitted to mention the extraordinary thing which had gone before. I desired to spare her all unnecessary terror.

"But, for myself, I had added an intolerable knowledge, to breed an incessant terror in my brain; for I doubted not but that I had seen the end of one of those men who had come to the island in the ship in the lagoon; and in that monstrous ending I had seen our own.

"Thereafter we kept from the abominable food, though the desire for it had entered into our blood. Yet our drear punishment was upon us; for, day by day, with monstrous rapidity, the fungoid growth took hold of our poor bodies. Nothing we could do would check it materially, and so — and so — we who had been human, became — Well, it matters less each day. Only — only we had been man and maid!

"And day by day the fight is more dreadful, to withstand the hunger-lust for the terrible lichen.

"A week ago we ate the last of the biscuit, and since that time I have caught three fish. I was out here fishing tonight when your schooner drifted upon me out of the mist. I hailed you. You know the rest, and may God, out of His great heart, bless you for your goodness to a — a couple of poor outcast souls."

There was the dip of an oar — another. Then the voice came again, and for the last time, sounding through the slight surrounding mist, ghostly and mournful.

"God bless you! Good-bye!"

"Good-bye," we shouted together, hoarsely, our hearts full of many emotions.

I glanced about me. I became aware that the dawn was upon us.

The sun flung a stray beam across the hidden sea; pierced the mist dully, and lit up the receding boat with a gloomy fire. Indistinctly I saw something nodding between the oars. I thought of a sponge — a great, grey nodding sponge —

The oars continued to ply. They were grey — as was the boat — and my eyes searched a moment vainly for the conjunction of hand and oar. My gaze flashed back to the — head. It nodded forward as the oars went backward for the stroke. Then the oars were dipped, the boat shot out of the patch of light, and the — the thing went nodding into the mist.

www.ingramcontent.com/pod-product-compliance
Lightning Source LLC
Chambersburg PA
CBHW020654180626
46816CB00003B/1274